DEMON ETERNAL

THE CAMELOT ARCHIVE - BOOK FOUR

NICOLE R. TAYLOR

Silver light shone down on the Darklands, casting long shadows over the nightmarish landscape.

Elijah and I ran through the crystalline maze, weaving around the enormous obsidian and smokey quartz points, our boots crunching against crumbled gemstones. I felt the eyes of the Old Ones on my back, their anger burning into my flesh. I'd killed one of their creatures and now I was an outlaw in a lawless land.

Only hours ago, the Celestial Morgana had pushed a relic—a fearsome predator with the head of a wolf, the antlers of a stag, and the body of a lion—through the veil into the Druid homeland where it proceeded to destroy everything in its path. I'd had two choices—let it carve through the Druid's homeland or kill it. I'd done what any warrior, Natural or otherwise, would have done—I stabbed it through its twin hearts.

Now we were on the way home, forced to run for

our lives because of my actions. If I'd let Elijah help, he would have broken the pact between the Druids and the Old Ones and been exiled for it. My place would always be on Earth, so it seemed worth the cost, despite our current flight through the Darklands.

Now, it was run or die.

There were creatures other than relics who patrolled this lightless place—shadows, spirits, and monsters so ancient no one had ever laid eyes on them. I could sense them all around, watching us, lingering just beyond the pale.

We paused at the edge of the rugged maze to catch our breath. The air was thick and the atmosphere pushed down on our shoulders like boulders. Everything was harder, even my abilities seemed a little farther away than usual.

I pressed my palm against stone, but it was cold to the touch. Like last time, I couldn't feel any warmth in this world. It teemed with dangerous life, even though scarce light touched its surface.

The laws that governed life as we knew it didn't seem to hold here and it made things all the more uncertain.

"Do we have to go as far as the forest?" I murmured, glancing at Elijah. It had taken us two days to find our way to Thríbhís Mhór, and I was dreading the way back.

"We can't just open the portal from anywhere," he reminded me. "We could end up on an alternate Earth…or inside a wall."

"So, it's back to the hill or nowhere at all."

He nodded. "We're making good time."

"Your Colours?"

He'd only just begun to recover them after the ritual at Briongló id Henge in the Druid homeland, Thríbhís Mhór. It would take time before they returned completely, but that was the thing about our predicament—we didn't have time to wait.

"They'll hold," he replied. "We just have to get the portal open."

Morgana was still out there and there was no telling when she might pop up. An immortal, borderline insane Celestial being was after us. It was Earth or bust. *Literally*.

"Can you feel that?" I rubbed my hand over the back of my neck and shivered.

Elijah scanned the forest ahead. "We better keep moving."

An enraged roar echoed from the maze behind us and we took off, not wanting to be anywhere near the crystals when the relics caught up to us. One was bad enough, but two? Three? A whole horde? Running sounded like a good idea.

We broke through the tree line and began to pick our way through the tangled woodland. Our progress was slow, hampered by centuries of unhindered growth. We'd traded one maze for another, but at least this one was familiar despite the black hue.

Hours passed, and I almost believed we were going to pass unhindered when my power began to zap through my veins. I was picking up on something that was growing in the shadows—figures, spirits, the empty husks known as the Unworthy.

Remembering our first trip here, and the lost souls the Darklands had claimed for its shadow army, I quickened my steps to catch up with Elijah.

He faltered in front of me and I knew he felt them, too. Still, I did the one thing people shouldn't do when they sensed something with murderous intent was stalking them.

I looked back.

Shadows swarmed after us like a thick cloud, wrapping around trees, oozing through gaps we had no hope of passing.

This was bad, but not just any bad. It was the *ultimate bad*.

We bolted, driven forwards by a primal need for survival. We hadn't come this far only to become empty husks.

Ahead, Elijah skidded as the shadow people poured over our path. He made a sharp right then leapt over a fallen log. I followed, my palm scraping on black lichen as I vaulted over the decaying tree.

There was no time to think, to cry out, to ask if he knew the way back to the hill. The shadows were on our tail and one misstep could see us overwhelmed. All we could do was run for our lives.

We swatted away thick vines and ducked underneath low hanging branches. I clambered over protruding roots and sharp rocks. We slipped along slimy black moss. Our breath quickened as the shadows closed in on us.

Just when I thought we'd become lost, we broke into clear ground, our boots thudding on springy pitch-coloured grass. Ahead, the ground began to rise into a clear sky.

The hill.

"Open the portal," I shouted to Elijah. "I'll hold them back!" He glanced over his shoulder, his eyes wild. *"I'm right behind you."*

Turning, I threw up my hands and cast a web of Light towards our pursuers. Gold shimmered brightly as the lost souls collided with it. The force of their blows shook the web, nearly knocking me over.

I felt Elijah call on his Colours, coaxing the portal to form, but without joining with my Druid Triune it wouldn't open completely.

Shadows gathered around my Light, scraping and clawing, sucking the power from my fingertips. I was keeping them from overwhelming us, but in doing so, I was giving them exactly what they needed to grow stronger.

We just needed enough time to open the portal. *Just a few more moments…*

"Madeleine!"

I grabbed Elijah's hand and our Colours linked. The portal snapped open and I let go of my Light. The web faded and shadows rushed us with unbelievable speed.

I wrapped my arms around Elijah, and with a burst of energy, I propelled us through the rippling surface and away from the Darklands.

We landed in a heap, rolling over cobblestones

and smashing into a wall. Behind us, the portal closed with a crack that forced my hands over my ears. Shadowy figures were sliced in half, dissipating into a cloud of black vapour. *Talk about a close call.*

I took a deep breath, my lungs filling with damp air, and turned to Elijah. Blood trickled down his forehead and he shook me away as I went to grasp his face so I could see how bad it was.

"I'm fine," he said. "It's just a scratch. We made it, that's all that matters."

Letting him have his way, I pushed to my feet and looked at where the portal had dumped us back on Earth.

We were in a house or ruin of some kind. Rubble lay everywhere, strewn across the room like something huge had smashed its way through the roof. Above, murky sunlight crept through, lighting the confined space.

I pressed my hand against my T-shirt, feeling for the crystal the Lady of the Lake had given me. It was still there, fastened in place by a silver chain. Inside the shard of clear quartz was a simple white flower. Almost identical to a forget-me-not, it was the only thing that could end a Celestial being's life.

Everything depended on this small bloom. *Such a simple thing.* If I'd lost it, defeat was imminent.

"Where are we?" I whispered, my voice bouncing off stone.

"Exactly where we left," Elijah replied. "Your parents' workshop."

I gasped and flattened my palms against the wall.

This was the last place I'd seen my parents alive. Morgana was bombarding South Bridge as we opened the portal, but they wouldn't come. Their research was more important. *They…*

"They made it out," Elijah said. "I know they did."

"How do you know?" The vault was full of rubble, but we'd landed in a pocket of space likely held open by the residue of the portal. At least, I hoped so. The roof looked like it was going to collapse at any moment.

He grimaced.

"*Elijah.*"

"There are no bodies," he said reluctantly.

I bit my tongue and began to search for a way out. We weren't far from the street, so I hoped there wasn't too far to go. I'd had more than enough for one day.

Together, we clawed our way through the rubble, pushing aside bluestone blocks with our powers. Elijah struggled with the unpredictable way his Colours were manifesting, but I helped him through.

Soon, we reached open air and clambered up to street level, but the rubble didn't end there. I stood on a block of sandstone, my gaze falling on an unfamiliar sight.

The destruction was catastrophic. South Bridge and the houses, shops, and bars which lined it had collapsed. The streets had been blocked off with temporary fencing and construction crews had already begun the arduous task of clearing away the debris.

Police and security personnel patrolled roadblocks, directing curious humans away from the scene. I stopped to read the signs fixed to the fencing, my heart breaking. *Danger. Do Not Enter: This area is unstable and may cause injury or death. Maximum penalties apply.*

I had no words. How could anyone survive this? The whole area was torn open. Not even in the eight hundred years the Naturals had warred with the Dark had things bled into the human world like this.

Tears stung my eyes as I wove a cloak around us. The reality of what we faced was setting in and guilt stabbed my heart.

"Madeleine," Elijah murmured, taking my hand.

"There's nothing left," I whispered, completely numb. "It's flattened. The whole bridge…"

He paused for a moment. "We can't linger."

I nodded, allowing him to help me down off the sandstone and through the temporary fencing. With my cloak wrapped around us, we passed unseen by the police officers who were pushing back curious humans.

"Clear the area," one officer shouted, "or I'll have to fine you for obstructing emergency services."

We began to move away from the scene, headed towards the outskirts of Edinburgh. Hanging around was a bad idea—the Dark could be watching.

Moving along Cowgate to Greyfriars, we approached the kirkyard, overly conscious that the ordinarily busy streets were empty. It was in this moment that I sensed the approach of something more than human.

In my shocked and exhausted state, I wasn't quite sure what it was. I drew my arondight blade and the links connected in a shower of silver and red sparks.

Elijah placed his hand on my shoulder. "It's okay," he whispered. "It's your parents."

I blinked, my heart skipping several beats as I caught sight of Bethany and Edward Greenbriar slinking out of a bin-lined Close, and my sword retracted.

The moment my mother wound her arms around my neck, I forgot all our past quarrels. Dad stood behind her and patted my shoulder, content to let her do all the hugging for him.

"*You made it*," I breathed.

"By the skin of our teeth," she said, drawing back. "Your father's Light saved us."

"The vault came down just after you went through the portal," he explained. "I had to cast a web to keep the ceiling from crushing us."

I blinked but couldn't picture it. "How did you get away from Morgana?"

"I think it was the residue from the portal that masked our escape."

"We kept our heads down, hoping you'd both reappear sooner or later," Mum added. "And here you are."

"We need to get off the street," Elijah said, looking at the sky. "Morgana could be watching for us."

"We're using a safe house in the south of the city,"

my father told us. "We'll make our way there and contact Camelot."

"We have a car," Mum said, ushering us down a tight close. "This way."

"Thank the Light," I said with a sigh. "We've been running for the last twenty-four hours."

"And the rest," Elijah added.

Mum glanced between us, her brow furrowing. "Dare I ask?"

I shook my head. "You wouldn't believe us even if we told you."

"We've spent our lives fighting demons from another world," she replied slowly. "I'd believe anything after all that."

As we disappeared amongst the streets of Edinburgh, I glanced at the sky, hoping the stars were looking the other way. If Morgana knew we'd returned, I didn't dare think about what she'd do when she found us.

I pressed my palm against the crystal flower. We were so close, yet so far.

The safe house was a small, unassuming cottage on the outskirts of Edinburgh.

Sitting at the table in the equally tiny kitchen, I watched Elijah shovel food into his mouth, stunned at his enthusiasm for scrambled eggs and beans.

"You're not hungry, Madeleine?" Mum asked as she held out the frying pan.

I shook my head. "I'm not hungry."

"Nonsense. You need to eat something."

I grimaced, knowing she wasn't going to like my explanation. "Ever since I became a Triune, my appetite isn't what it used to be."

Her smile faded. "Oh…"

Dad gestured to her and held out his plate. "I'll finish the eggs off, sweetheart."

Elijah looked up from his breakfast and offered me a half-smile as my mother sat a teacup of the in front of me. We might be Naturals, but we were still English.

"Did you find the Druids?" Dad asked. "I assume you did because you made your way back." He gave Elijah a knowing look.

"My Colours are returning," he told them. "Slowly, but they were still there."

"And the Lady of the Lake?" Mum asked as she sat down.

"I met her," I replied.

Dad's fork stopped halfway into his mouth and a sliver of egg slipped and plopped onto the table.

"It's a long story," I muttered. A long story I simply didn't have the strength to tell. My mind was firmly locked on the crystal hanging beneath my T-shirt.

"Well," Elijah said. "The long and the short of it is…"

I cradled the cup against my chest as he gave my parents the abridged version of our time away. I tuned out, my mind going back to the destruction at South Bridge. A flower could stop all that? I just didn't get it.

"What are the newspapers saying?" I asked, abruptly interrupting Dad's incessant questioning about the Darklands.

"The media is reporting it as another earthquake," Mum told me. "Their scientists are trying to link the activity to the volcano."

"After Morgana made the magma rise, they just might find their evidence," Dad added. "At least the truth of what the world faces is still a secret. The last thing we need is military response."

"Or disclosure," Mum declared. "If humanity learned of the supernatural, I loathe to think what will happen to us."

Elijah grunted. "Live autopsies."

I was only half-listening, but his wry joke brought me back. "Trust you to say that."

"Has there been any other activity?" the Druid asked.

"None," Dad replied. "Things have gone quiet, but Greer might have more to say on the matter. We've been isolated from most of the goings-on up here."

"How many," I whispered.

"How many what?" Dad asked with a frown.

"Lives," I snarled. "How many lives were lost at the bridge?"

He glanced at my mother. "Eight with fifty-three taken to hospital with minor injuries."

My blood ran cold and I wasn't sure if I was going to explode or crumble.

"It could have been much worse," Mum told me. "Once the tremors began, people evacuated."

"It doesn't matter," I cried. "We're supposed to protect them. *One life is too many*."

"We couldn't have stopped her, even if we tried," Elijah said, laying his hand on mine. "We have a chance to end this for good, but we can't stop everything."

"Bad things are going to happen," Dad murmured. "We all grew up with war, sweetheart. It's not nice, but losses are to be expected."

"To be expected?" I scoffed, slamming my cup of tea onto the table. Brown liquid sloshed over the edge, pooling on the wood.

"Madeleine," Mum began, but Elijah gestured for her to calm.

"Let's take a breath," he said, ever the voice of reason. "We'll contact Camelot and let them know we made it. We'll return as soon as we can. I think we might feel better amongst friends."

"And behind an illusion, a barrier, and a small army," Mum added. "It's no Avalon, but it just might be the next best thing."

I gritted my teeth and rose to my feet. Everyone was staring at me, waiting to see what I'd say—or if I'd explode.

I didn't know what it was about this world, but I felt disconnected here. In Thríbhís Mhór, I fed off the calm and simple way the Druids lived and thrived. Here, even within the denseness of the city, my anxiety was off the charts. It was a far cry from the days I longed to patrol the streets of London fighting demons.

I was born a Natural, but now I was a Triune, and I felt more in tune with the Druids. I wondered why that was.

"I need some air," I said, snapping back into reality. The cottage was so small, the air was stifling.

"Madeleine, we know this is a difficult time—" Mum began.

"I'm not angry at you," I interrupted. "I just…

The last week has been a lot to deal with." I swallowed hard and pushed out the backdoor.

Outside, the garden was a tangle of weeds and thistles. If there'd been any flowers or lawn, it was a long time since either had seen the fleeting Scottish sun. Landscaping was low on the Naturals' priority list. First came demon hunting. Second came demon hunting. There was only one way the list went, and weeding didn't rate a mention.

The door opened behind me and I sensed Elijah as he edged through the gap. He stood beside me, frowning at the state of the garden. Plants were a Druid thing.

"I know I'm taking this way too hard…" I began, but he shook his head.

"You aren't."

"Then why aren't you upset?"

"We are upset, but we can't let it consume us."

"Innocent people died because we needed a portal. It seems selfish to me."

"Morgana killed them," he told me. "We did everything we could."

"The Codex preaches about love and honour, and the Twin Flames had to merge with nothing but true love in their hearts, but I can't see it. We're still human at our core."

"You're not human," he murmured. "And neither am I."

I scowled and shook my head. "I'm one-third Natural, and Naturals were created from humanity."

Elijah watched me carefully, his Colours stirring. It

felt like he was sifting through my emotions, searching for something.

"Stop that," I snapped.

He sighed and moved closer. "You're afraid the Naturals are going to blame you for what happened at the bridge."

I looked away, focusing my gaze on the bottom of the garden. With my history, how could I not? I was uncomfortable in my own skin before I became a Triune, and afterwards, it seemed amplified. The only thing I knew was fighting, but even that was beyond me after seeing the cost of war at South Bridge.

"I'm trying to be strong, like—" I clamped my mouth shut. *Like Scarlett.* "But I'm not."

"You are strong, Madeleine. You don't have to be like anyone else," he murmured. "Only you could have gotten this far, and it's not because of what you've become, but *who*. A few weeks ago, you couldn't even tell me how you felt. Now…" His fingertips grazed over my arm where his prism warmed my skin.

"It's just… That time away in the homeland made everything seem so far away and the first thing we see when we come back is death and destruction. It was terrible and that was nothing compared to what she could do to the entire world. It shocked me, Elijah. Knowing and seeing are so different."

"The Lady of the Lake trusts you," he said. "She knows this fight isn't going to be easy, and we can't expect it to be, either. We have to keep moving and face it with courage."

"I'm tired of fighting," I whispered.

"So am I," he replied. "*So am I.*"

I sucked in a deep breath, relishing the light air of Earth and the crispness of the Scottish Lowlands. Winter was upon us, and snow would soon follow. What a time to be fighting with fire.

"Well," I said, "at least my parents seem to like you now."

Elijah laughed and ran his hand over his face. "Well, we have to start somewhere."

"Like going back to Camelot as soon as possible?"

"Madeleine, we haven't rested in days," he said. "Not since the night before the ritual."

"I feel fine," I declared.

"I know you just want the best for everyone, but…" Elijah's lips thinned. "It's been a long time since… Well, I'm not used to it, is all."

I hesitated, realisation hitting me square in the face. Elijah wasn't as powerful as he had been as a demon-hybrid, nor was he anywhere near his full strength as a Druid. We'd been through so much in the past six months, I'd forgotten all about his struggles. *I was so selfish.*

"I'm sorry," I said with a groan. "I forget how much you've been through. I'm an epic bitch."

"You're focused on Morgana. I get it."

"It's not an excuse." I cupped his face in my hand, my thumb scratching over his stubbled jaw. "I've pushed you too far."

His lips quirked. "Just remember some of us have to stop to eat and sleep."

The cottage was cloaked with a thousand layers of wards and illusions that had been built up over time. There was little chance we'd be found, unless someone knew where to look. If Morgana was searching for us, it would be like trying to find a needle in a haystack. At least, I hoped that was the case.

"We've got a moment," Elijah added. "Studying that flower is going to take time. Besides, we need a strategy if we're going to use it."

"You've got a point."

"I *am* a Druid," he declared. "Man, it feels good to say it like that."

"With certainty?" I smiled and felt his Colours brush against my matching Triune.

He nodded. "Oh, and Edward is on the phone with Camelot now. They'll expect us tomorrow or the day after."

I raised my eyebrows. "Oh, so it's *Edward* now. Not Mr. Greenbriar."

"I like to think he's into me because of my wit and charm, not my portal opening Colours."

"Me too," I said as he ushered me inside. "Me too."

I lay in an unfamiliar bed, staring at an unfamiliar ceiling. The sheets were scratchy and smelt a little musty. I narrowed my eyes at the small silver Lady of the Lake statue that sat on the mantle over the fireplace. The Celestial was just as difficult as Merlin when it came to explaining things. No one could give anyone straight answers—it was always about the *journey*.

I was so tired of 'journeys'.

Elijah lay beside me, his chest rising and falling as he slept. My eyes drooped, lulled by his complete lack of snoring. *How did I get so lucky?* A boyfriend with clear sinuses was like finding a unicorn fart in the wind.

The room shimmered, my vision sparkled with stars, and I cursed under my breath. Shenanigans were afoot and my arondight blade was on the floor, just out of reach.

Elijah had told me once that I didn't need a sword to fight. A sword was a tool, not the source of my power—it came from within, from my soul.

I sat up, squinting as the walls began to melt away. A valley appeared before me and I climbed out of bed, my feet burying into soft, springy grass. *I am not afraid.*

I was in Avalon.

Blinking, I turned to find Elijah and the bed were gone.

"I knew sleep would take you sooner or later."

The Lady of the Lake's voice tricked over me like crystalline water and I looked over my shoulder. She was sitting on the edge of a stone, looking over the valley to the lake beyond. Her silver hair fluttered in the breeze, sparkling like it was woven with a trillion diamonds.

I closed my eyes for a moment and said a silent prayer. Just one good night's sleep was all I asked.

Sighing, I went and sat beside her. Who was I to deny the creator of the Naturals? She was a Celestial being, after all. Granted, she wasn't Morgana, but her power was just as palpable.

"I'm having another one of those freaky dreams again, aren't I?" I asked, overly conscious I was wearing only a T-shirt and underpants. "The kind were I'm really talking to my subconscious."

"Perhaps…" she said. "There's something you need to understand, but does it really matter how the truth is delivered?"

"I stopped wondering about those things months ago," I told her. "I used to live in an extraordinary world, now I live in… well, whatever comes after that."

The Lady smiled, her skin shimmering with translucent stardust.

"If I'd known you were going to call, I would have put on some trousers."

"To talk to your subconscious?"

"You make an excellent point."

Together, we watched the light play across Ynys Wydryn—the Isle of Glass. Whatever it was I had to understand via this little dream was beyond me, but I was glad to remember Avalon. It was such a beautiful, *peaceful* place.

"I've been on Earth less than a day and I'm already moody," I mused. "Why is that?"

"Your Light and Dark Triunes are at war with one

another," the Lady replied. "In your world, it has always been thus. In Thríbhís Mhór, there has only been peace for the Druids."

"That explains a lot."

"You already understood this, Madeleine."

"And there's the punchline," I scoffed and clapped my hands together. "What else do I need to know?"

She smiled and picked up a strand of my black hair. "You tell me."

"You came to Earth once before." I didn't know where the statement came from, but something inside me wanted to say it.

"A thousand years before Camelot," she said. "When the first Naturals rose."

"Were you here after that? Or was Avalon always where you lived?"

"I came to Earth many times to see how my children were faring," she replied. "The last time… I broke a pact I vowed to uphold for eternity…" I wondered if I was still speaking to my mind or to the Lady herself. It was difficult to tell what was real these days.

"When I was in Avalon, you said you could watch over me."

"*Watch*," she said firmly.

"I thought I was dreaming, but… I hoped this was…" My heart sank. "You're not really here, are you?"

"What is real, Madeleine? Is it what your mind perceives or what your eyes see? Or is it something else?"

"I can see why you and Merlin get along so well," I drawled.

"He keeps my mind sharp."

"When was the last time you were on Earth?" I wondered out loud. "Before or after Arthur put Morgana in the vault?"

The Lady of the Lake rose, her white dress falling into place like liquid silk.

"It's time to wake now, Madeleine," she murmured. "Camelot is calling."

3

____

When Elijah and I arrived at Edinburgh Waverley station the next morning, it was teeming with peak-hour commuters.

After we'd had a long argument with my parents about the pros and cons of splitting up, we left the cottage, determined to take the next train headed south to Wales. I didn't like it, but Elijah said it was for the best. Too many people moving together was a risk, especially when the Dark was looking for us. We were a high-priority target for Morgana's minions and having my parents with us only put them in unnecessary danger.

I would have liked to have taken the car but despite our issues, I wanted my parents behind the barrier at Camelot as soon as possible. I'd made a promise to work things out with them when I faced the Old Ones trial in the Darklands, and I intended to see it through…just as I had with Elijah.

We wove through the swarm of humans walking

over the overpass, looking for a timetable. Footsteps echoed as the black and grey swarm of office workers and school kids merged towards the exits or down towards the platforms. I watched them pass, thinking how dull it must be to sit in front of a computer and send emails and invoices all day.

Overhead, automated announcements blared out of speakers. *"The next train to depart from platform four is the eight-forty-five ScotRail service to Glasgow Central, stopping at Haymarket, Linlithgow…"*

Tugging on Elijah's sleeve, I led him down a flight of stairs and onto the main concourse where a large display of departures glowed, attracting humans like moths to a flame.

I scanned the garish orange display, looking for something that passed by Camelot. The list of trains was long, with services leaving every few minutes for places all over Scotland and farther afield in the United Kingdom.

"There," I said. "The Virgin Trains service to London Euston stops close to Camelot."

"We can get off at Crewe and get a local train to Church Stretton," Elijah said. Church Stretton was a village in the centre of the Clee Hills and a short car ride away from the hidden ruins of Camelot. It was a quaint market town full of antique shops, tea rooms, and bed and breakfasts. Before all the trouble with the archive, it was one of the places the Naturals used to frequent.

"I'm not going to ask how you know so much

about Welsh trains," I quipped. "But the quicker we can get there, the better."

"Church Stretton is an old place," he added. "It goes back to the Romans and even further to the Iron Age. There's a hill fort on Caer Caradoc."

I knew why he was so knowledgeable about the area around Camelot and wasn't sure if I should be outraged on his behalf. Ikakantor's memory was long and the Dark had held the city for centuries before we'd won it back. It wouldn't help us to open old wounds, so I turned my attention onto the comings and goings of the station.

Commuters rushed to platforms and scanned their tickets. Barriers squealed as they opened and banged as they shut. People lingered at the departure displays, waiting for their trains to be announced, while others milled around the *Pret a Manger* sandwich shop or circled the *WH Smith* for magazines and sweets.

"I don't like this," I muttered, my gaze flickering from face to face. "There's too many people."

"There's more humans than there are demons," Elijah replied. "As long as we keep our heads down, they won't even know we're here."

I snorted. "The invisibility cloak helps."

"Ready for some fare evasion?" He smirked and nodded towards the display where our platform number had appeared.

"No time like the present to add to my rap sheet."

"There's no room left on mine," he quipped.

"You always have to do one better, don't you?" I

complained as we walked across the overpass and found our train.

"I'm feeling confident."

"Don't get too carried away. Remember what Merlin told you."

"I know," Elijah snorted as we walked along the platform looking for a quiet carriage. "I won't push my Colours too hard."

I didn't want to know what would happen if he stretched a little too far. Hopefully it was a hurdle he wouldn't have to face—as long as he heeded Merlin's advice.

"Here," I murmured, keeping my voice low. "This one is as good as any."

Elijah waited for a woman to board before stepping in behind her. I followed, peering down the aisle, scanning the humans inside.

I could sense nothing untoward and hoped it was an omen. *So far, so good.*

We lingered in the compartment at the end of the carriage, leaning against the opposite door. A few stragglers passed by, unaware of us as they loaded up luggage onto the racks and moved through the train to find their allocated seats.

Outside, the platform attendant blew their whistle, signalling our imminent departure. The doors closed and the train began to pull away from the platform. I leaned against the window, watching as the station fell away and the city began to appear. Edinburgh was beautiful. I just wished we hadn't left the mark on it that we had.

"How long does it take to get to Crewe?" I asked.

"About four hours. There's a lot of stops on this line."

I sighed and looked around the little compartment. A toilet was on one side and the luggage rack on the other. We stood in the alcove by the doors, unable to find a seat because of our current invisibility.

"You can run for a whole day with hardly stopping, but you can't stand on a train for four hours?" He was taking the piss, but I narrowed my eyes.

"It's not so much the standing as the lack of exit strategy," I told him. "But I don't like being still, so take your pick."

"Standing in one place is exhausting."

"It *so* is," I declared. "I wonder why?"

"Movement creates energy, while standing drains reserves."

"Perpetual motion?" I wondered.

"Perpetual motion violates the laws of thermodynamics," Elijah stated. "No machine or biological matter can work forever without inputting energy. At least, at some point. It's a myth."

I raised my eyebrows. When did he have the time to learn this stuff? I shook my head, realising he'd had eight centuries to learn whatever he wanted.

Sensing my indifference to his scientific ramblings, he turned his attention to the window where Edinburgh had given way to the rolling green hills of the Scottish Lowlands.

A newspaper was sticking out of the rubbish bin and I pulled it free, my touch rendering it invisible to anyone outside of our cloak. Elijah looked over my shoulder, reading as I smoothed the crease out of the front page.

The Lord Provost of Edinburgh, William McDougall, has called for a citywide building survey to be competed following the recent earthquakes that rocked the city. "In the interest of public safety and preserving the rich heritage of our capital, we must do whatever is in our power to ensure that the collapse of South Bridge does not happen again," he said. On the unrest that occurred between police and victims' families yesterday at the scene, he commented, "I ask for all residents to abide with the directions given by our emergency services. They are here to help, not hinder."

"Things are really messed up…" I murmured.

"It can't be helped," Elijah said. "You should turn to the celebrity gossip."

I turned and gave him an incredulous look. "*Celebrity gossip?*"

"Yeah. I want to see who's dissing who on social media."

I pressed my finger to my lips as the conductor—a woman with authoritatively thin lips—strode past us and into the next carriage.

As soon as she was gone, Elijah took the newspaper from me and flipped to the centre so he could get his gossip fix.

We remained like this for the next few hours, watching as humans got on and off while cities and countryside rolled by. We spotted ruined castles, Elijah pointed out ancient hill forts, and everything seemed to go smoothly until I felt the telltale pull of Darkness.

The doors between carriages hissed as they opened and a man walked though, passing us and disappearing into the aisle.

There wasn't anything extraordinary about him—he was a stocky, bald, middle-aged Englishman wearing jeans and a bomber jacket—but he wasn't alone. I could sense the creature possessing the innocent and bristled. *Infernal.* It was in that man, but it could hop into anyone at any time and no one would be any the wiser.

It must have gotten on at the last stop, slinking onto the train in a carriage towards the end. The cloak only went as far as human eyes, not demon ones. Thanks to my Triune, I *did* have the unique ability to render myself invisible to supernatural eyes, but there were loopholes I couldn't always control. I didn't think it'd seen us when it passed, but I couldn't be sure.

I couldn't take the chance that my ability hadn't faltered. If we moved or drew attention to ourselves, it would know what we were. Our arondight blades were hidden, but the black tactical trousers and matching jackets stuck out like a sore thumb.

Elijah glanced at me and I slipped my hand into his. If they were watching the trains, then they must know we'd returned. There was no other reason why it'd be here unless it was a rogue demon out to cause havoc on its own, though I doubted it.

The Lady of the Lake had told me that Morgana

had created the Dark. Now that she'd risen again, she would have called all her creatures to her in preparation to play out her revenge. It really would be the war to end all wars if it came to an all-out battle.

"We can't let it get to her," Elijah whispered.

"I know, but we can't be sure it's seen us yet. Besides, this is a bad place to have a showdown."

The train doors were sealed, only opening when the driver disengaged them at a station. Unless I slammed my fist down onto the emergency stop button, we weren't getting off any time soon.

"We have to sit tight," I whispered. "See where it goes."

"If it wants to fight, then what?" Elijah asked. "There's too many people on the train, let alone a station."

"What's the next stop?"

"Warrington."

I cursed under my breath. We still had another station before Crewe. Couldn't anything go right for once? Just a smooth ride back to Camelot would have been *everything*, but no…

"I think we should get off at the next stop," Elijah said. "If it follows, we can deal with it then and there. We can find another way to Camelot. I know how to hot-wire a car, you know."

"I'm sure you do," I muttered as I looked down the aisle.

"If you use your Triune abilities, Morgana will know where we are," he warned.

I brushed my palm over the hilt of my cold iron

dagger. "Then we'll have to do this the Natural way—with an old-fashioned exorcism."

We were going to have to lure it away from the city into a quiet corner where we could jump it without bringing any more innocents into the mix.

The train eased into the platform of Warrington Bank Quay, coming to a gentle stop. The area didn't look that busy, though people were waiting to get on. As the door opened and passengers got off, I stepped forwards and caught our target's eye. I gave him a little wave, then jumped off the train with Elijah on my heels.

A commotion erupted behind us as the demon followed, shoving people out of the way in its haste to keep up.

We leapt down onto the tracks and onto the opposite platform with the demon chasing us. Jumping the fence, we legged it down the street and found ourselves by a river with a factory at our backs.

Sensing Darkness right behind us, I decided this was as good a place as any and drew my cold iron dagger.

I skidded to a stop and held out my arm. The man slammed into me and the momentum and my Light-braced arm flipped him over. As he landed on his back, I stabbed the blade through his shoulder. His flesh hissed, steaming as the metal reacted to the parasite hidden inside his body.

The demon screeched, thrashing against the dagger, but it was stuck. I drove the blade deeper and called on my Light, reinforcing our cloak and beginning the first stages of getting its claws out of the human.

"*Prize et mortale*," I chanted, beginning to break the parasite's hold, "*hoc a te carnem—*"

The words died in my throat as a second demon appeared behind us and lunged at me with a fistful of Darkness. It wasn't an Infernal or a lesser demon—it was one of the twisted creatures that survived Camelot, which meant I was right about them watching the trains. Its appearance wasn't great for my exorcism, though.

I reached for my arondight blade with my left hand, but I knew I wasn't going to be quick enough to counterstrike.

Elijah leapt in front of the demon, a pulse of Colour wrapping around his hand. It flared into a prism as they collided, and the blue shards speared into its black hide.

The demon shrieked as it burst into flames and I was torn between the Druid and the Infernal on the ground.

Elijah fell to his knees, a painful cry tearing from his lips as his Colours erupted. Holographic shards exploded outward, forming contorted crystalline shapes, reflecting a rainbow of blue, silver, and green. It was beautiful and horrifying all at the same time.

My moment of indecision gave the demon enough time to wrench the cold iron dagger from its chest and regain its footing. My Druid Triune flared, and I turned to face it.

"It's only a matter of time," the man rasped. "The Dark will rise again."

"I don't think so," I hissed. "Not on my watch."

"Filthy, Triune. You have no idea what she is capable of."

I sneered, "All I care about right now is destroying you."

The man's lip curled and the Infernal reached for its Darkness. If it used its power against me, the human's mind would be fried. I had to make a choice and make it fast.

I lunged, phasing out of my body and into the ether—just like I had back in Edinburgh when Morgana had found me. I didn't understand what I was doing, but I had no choice. Elijah was on the brink of collapse, his Colours building towards critical mass.

Time ebbed to a standstill and I saw the Darkness wrapped around the neck and spine of the human. Red barbs dug into his brain, forging the connection between parasite and host.

My spirit rushed at it, and I plunged my ethereal fist into the man's chest. Grasping the invader, I wrenched it from him and tore apart the essence with an angry roar.

There were no fames or explosions, but I knew it was gone. Destroying its spirit had caused the creature to cease to be.

I stepped backwards with a gasp and pushed back into my body. Time sped up and the man crumpled to the ground, unconscious. He'd be fine, but we couldn't leave him on the street like this.

"Elijah?" When he didn't reply, I turned to find him kneeling on the ground, shaking. "Elijah, we have to move. I had to use my powers to stop the demon. Morgana will know where we are."

He fisted his hands into his hair.

"*Elijah.*"

"I can't stop it," he cried. "Madeleine, you have to—"

I realised what was happening a split-second before all hell broke loose.

Elijah wailed as his Colours exploded and I threw my arms around him, pouring all three of my Triunes into his body. I covered him in Light, wrapped him in Colour, and sealed it with Darkness, hoping it would be enough to contain the blast.

Energy built up around the Druid, pulsing and pouring from his mouth and eyes, splinters of unformed prisms tearing through his body.

"*Hold on,*" I cried, pushing against my limits. "I won't leave you…"

I sensed him trying to contain the overload, but his soul screamed as his grip loosened.

The world shattered…

And everything went dark.

4

It wasn't my finest moment, but the next thing I did was steal a car.

A human man was lingering in the factory car park, smoking and scrolling one-handed on his smartphone. I stole that, too—the phone, not the cigarettes.

It'd been a long time since I'd used alteration on a human. I never used to feel bad about manipulating their minds when it was in the name of demon hunting, but after everything I'd been through since the summer, my conscious was overgrowing.

By some miracle, I'd been able to contain the blast from Elijah's overload and kept our position concealed from the world. Problem was, we were stranded. We couldn't get another train and public phone boxes had gone out of style twenty years ago.

I thought about the scorch mark we'd left behind on the outskirts of Warrington and cursed Merlin for not warning us about a potential Colour bomb going off.

I glanced at Elijah, who sat in the passenger seat, staring blankly out the front window. He hadn't said a word since his Colours spiked. Whatever had happened, it had rendered him nearly catatonic.

I couldn't blame him, but I knew when he came around, he'd be devastated. He'd only been trying to save my life.

"I should have known there was another one," I said. "I was too focused on the Infernal."

Elijah didn't reply.

I frowned, worried that he was withdrawing too far. I could go into his mind again, to see if I could draw him out, but I couldn't risk it here. Camelot was our safest bet.

I drove us out of the city, pulling into the first rest stop along the motorway. I parked the car in a quiet corner of the lot behind the *Shell Service Station* and climbed out into the freezing air.

Taking out the stolen phone, I glanced at Elijah through the windscreen. *Why didn't he just use his arondight blade?*

Thankfully, the phone wasn't passcode locked, so I punched in the number I remembered as Issac's. He was just about the only Natural in Camelot who had one.

"Hello?" His voice was a welcome sound in a sea of chaos.

"Issac? It's Madeleine."

"Madeleine?" He sounded relieved. "We were

expecting you hours ago."

"I know. We ran into a little problem," I said. "The train was compromised, and we had to ditch it."

"Where are you now?"

"Near Chester," I told him. "I've found us a car, but I had to steal it. Are my parents back yet?"

"They arrived a few hours ago," he replied.

"Good. I…" I took a deep breath. "Issac. Something happened. An Infernal chased us from the train and I had to use my Triune to… well, I tried to do an exorcism, but there was another demon and Elijah—" I swallowed hard. "He used his Colours to kill it, but it was too much too soon… I—"

"Take a breath," he said with a worried voice. "Where is Elijah now?"

"He's in the car, but he's not *there*." I glanced at the car where the Druid hadn't moved an inch since I'd fastened his seatbelt. "His Colours exploded and it took everything I had to contain the blast. I had to use my abilities and now Morgana knows we're back and I—" I choked back a sob.

"You were only following protocol," he reassured me. "Don't blame yourself, Madeleine."

"Why didn't he just use his arondight blade?" I muttered.

"Did you say Elijah's Colours are back?"

"They were. I mean…I think they still are. I really don't know."

A rustling sound echoed down the phone. "Sit tight, I'm going to send some back-up."

"We're fine. It's not that far to Camelot." I focused

on Elijah and my anxiety began to spike.

"Madeleine, I'm glad you're back in our world but you need help. There's no shame in taking it, even if you're the Triune."

"*The* Triune?"

"You're the only one, aren't you?"

I sighed, my exhaustion beginning to catch up with me. Maybe I'd used more power trying to contain Elijah's Colours than I thought I had. *I was not a Flame. I was not infinite.*

"Watch for us," I said. "I'll take the most direct route back to Camelot."

"Madel—"

I ended the call and slid back into the car. Elijah continued to stare, though he blinked once, the tiny movement fostering a spark of hope.

What did Merlin say about knots? "*If you are set on returning, Caradhan, then be warned. Without a connection to Thríbhís Mhór, your Colours may overwhelm you. They have been subdued for a long time and their return will be unpredictable. I have guided you as much as I can. If it happens, there is nothing to be done but wait for you to work your way through the knot.*"

Who was I to question Merlin? There was nothing I could do but protect Elijah until he worked out the knot of Colour inside his spirit.

I slammed the car into drive and peeled out of the car park, swerving around the corner and back onto the motorway. Camelot was the safest place for the both of us—including the flower hanging around my neck.

And the sooner we got there, the better.

———

It was dark when I finally drove through the gates of Camelot, the barrier shimmering gold as the car passed the outer defences.

Elijah and I had been gone a little over a week, and in that time, no one had been idle. The city had been fortified up to the proverbial eyeballs.

The wall was manned with a double detail of Naturals, the walls were reinforced with Light, trenches had been dug around the base camp, and prefabricated buildings to house extra personnel had been erected in record speed.

Where infrastructure had been lacking, the Naturals had brought it with them. Water tanks, generators, supplies, vehicles, portable toilets—if I could think of it, they probably had it trucked in.

The headlights illuminated Ramona and Issac, who came to meet us as I brought the car to a stop.

Ramona opened the passenger door and knelt beside Elijah. Checking his pulse, she frowned and gestured to me. "How long has he been like this?"

"A few hours. Three at the most."

Ramona clucked her tongue, looking worried.

"Merlin said he might encounter this," I told her.

Her eyes widened. "Merlin?"

I filled her in on what the Druid had explained to us before Elijah and I left the homeland.

"Well, his body is reactive," she mused. "His

mind… If it's as you say, then we just have to keep him comfortable." She unclipped the seatbelt and coaxed the Druid out of the car. "C'mon, you. Let's get you inside where it's warm." As he stood, she set her hand on the top of his head to stop him from hitting it on the way up.

I climbed out of the car and Issac stood beside me, taking the keys out of my hand. I watched Ramona lead Elijah to the infirmary, torn between following them and the weight of the flower around my neck.

"She'll look after him," Issac said. "I know you don't want to leave his side, but your health is important, too."

"And my report," I drawled, glancing at him. It was good to see a familiar face again, even though he seemed more concerned with what we'd found rather than Elijah's health.

"Yes, of course." He grimaced, but I knew he had to ask. That was our predicament, after all. "Did you find what you were looking for?"

I nodded.

"*Thank the Light.*"

"Really?" I raised my eyebrows. "I seem to remember you weren't that fussed on us going in the first place."

"I see you've lost none of your straightforward charm."

"It's been a week and a half, not a thousand years," I huffed.

"Madeleine, you went to the Druid homeland," he

argued. "That in itself is extraordinary, but to see Avalon and speak with the Lady of the Lake?" His eyes widened. "I wish I could have been there with you."

I didn't know what to say, so I shrugged. I wasn't so sure he'd be jealous when he heard about the relics.

"There's so much I need to tell you," I murmured.

"Best tell it when Greer is here," he said. "I know how you hate repeating yourself." I managed to crack a smile and he chuckled. "That's what I like to see."

"I would have thought she would be in London, or somewhere less in the blast radius," I said.

"Greer is needed here despite the danger, but the Codex has been moved to a secure location. London isn't safe." He placed his hand on the small of my back and guided me towards camp.

"What about Wilder and Scarlett?"

"Relocated to a secret facility."

I raised my eyebrows but he didn't elaborate. The less people who knew, the better...especially me. I was at the top of Morgana's most wanted list and I couldn't forget the first time we met up at the castle. She dove into my mind and taken everything I knew. Nothing was a secret if she got her hands on any one of us.

"Every Sanctum and outpost are on lockdown," Issac went on. "Everyone who can be spared has been transferred to Camelot."

"Is that wise?" Putting all our forces in one place wasn't the best strategic move, considering how few of us were left after the war.

"We're constantly on the move," he explained. "Base camp is the only permanent fixture in the city and surrounding hills. Camelot has its defences, but there's still too few of us to protect the entire perimeter all at once."

"Have there been any sightings?"

He shook his head. "Apart from a few skirmishes with the ex-Camelot demons, nothing. The last encounter with Morgana was at South Bridge."

I froze, the memory of the collapsed bridge grating against my heart.

Issac sensed my anxiety and pulled me into the shadow of a building, away from prying eyes.

"Those deaths weren't your fault," he murmured. "Neither was the volcano."

"We could have moved the portal to a safe house or somewhere outside the city," I argued. "It was reckless to even attempt it in the city centre. Just because we're supernatural, doesn't mean we have to be arrogant about it. This is the human's world, Issac. We just protect it."

His brow furrowed and he grasped my shoulders. "It's our world, too."

I lowered my gaze. Maybe the pressure was finally getting to me.

"C'mon," Issac said. "Greer will want to hear what intel you have…that is, if you're up to it."

I had little choice in the matter. "Then we better get going. What I've got to say will rock your world, Worthington."

He chuckled softly. "Oh, it's like that, is it?"

I gave him a pointed look. "*And more.*"

———

The Regula had set up a command post in a plain, unassuming prefabricated building in the centre of base camp.

Guards were posted at the door, along with wards and barriers which had been thickly layered around the entire structure. They had a familiar flair to them, reminding me of Masters. The last time I'd seen him was the day the vault exploded.

"These are Masters' wards?" I asked, glancing at Issac.

He nodded. "He's doing much better. Morgana really wore his mind down, but we've helped him gain his strength back."

"Good." I studied the barrier as he opened the door for me. "I'm glad. He was the best Light Studies teacher I had at the Academy."

"He was the *only* Light Studies teacher you ever had," Issac said with a smirk. "The man's taught there for twenty years."

"Madeleine." Greer's voice drew my attention into the room, and I blinked in surprise as she embraced me, her touch light and angelic. "It's good to see you back in Camelot."

"It seems like forever since I've been here," I told her. "So much has changed."

"We've been hard at work building our defences." She gestured for me and Issac to sit at the table.

"Aiden will be glad. He's had a great deal of trouble reconstructing the vault. Whatever the Naturals did to build it all that time ago is a mystery. No one can figure it out."

Issac nodded. "It's like trying to understand how Stonehenge was built."

"The Druids," I said as I looked around the command post.

Maps and diagrams hung all over the walls, along with photographs and other reconnaissance. The table was large enough to seat twelve, with matching chairs. Other than that, it was largely empty and cold to look at. Everything was white and grey.

"The Druids?" Greer inquired.

"They had a henge that was exactly like it, only three times the size. Brionglóid."

"Reverie," Issac murmured. "A place of dreaming…"

I nodded as I sat at the table and folded my hands into my lap. He would have thrived amongst the Druids with their spiritual ways.

"How is Elijah?" Greer asked.

"Withdrawn," I replied. "His Colours were restored, but they overwhelmed him. He just… Merlin called it a *knot*. He'll have to work it out himself. I—" I shook my head as my heart ached. Knowing I was powerless to help him didn't sit well with who I was as a warrior. All I knew how to do was fight.

"I know you've been through a great deal,

Madeleine," Greer began, "but we have to know what you found."

"I understand. We're up against a lot." I wiggled my backside on my chair. "You better get comfortable. It's a tale and a half." I took a deep breath and told them everything.

From Morgana's sadistic experiments with the volcano in Edinburgh, my parents' portal, South Bridge, the flight through the Darklands with the shadows and relic, Elijah's sister Eliorla and the *neach-gleidhidh*—the Druid guardians, the Old Ones, and Merlin, and Avalon and the Lady of the Lake. I recounted the story of the Celestials' beginning and why they couldn't exist in the same world along with Scarlett and Wilder.

Finally, I explained that Morgana had created the Dark out of her lust for power and domination, and how Merlin and Arthur had worked with the Lady to seal her inside the vault, hoping she could be redeemed. We all knew that imprisonment had only caused the Celestial to grow more unpredictable. There was only one way to end all of this and save Earth and Thríbhís Mhór.

With Morgana's death.

Thanks to the Lady of the Lake, I had the key to the Celestial's demise hanging around my neck. I took it out, the crystal-encased flower spinning as I held it up for Issac and Greer to see.

"This is what's going to end her," I said as they stared at the tiny flower, equal parts transfixed and confused. "And now you know as much as I do."

"A flower?" Issac asked.

"The Lady said they grew where the Celestials walked," I replied. "And when the relic came through to Thríbhís Mhór, it broke Morgana's hold long enough so I could kill it. The ground swallowed the corpse whole and they sprouted where it lay." I set the crystal onto the table. "I don't know why or how, but this is what she gave me."

They were silent for a long time, their thoughts hidden from me. I knew how it looked. I was expecting a nuclear bomb but was given a pebble instead. There *was* power in its petals—I'd seen the proof.

Finally, it was Greer who reached out and picked up the crystal. She held it aloft, studying the bloom suspended inside the clear quartz.

"We now know Morgana isn't as absolute as she thinks she is," she murmured. "She can't sense you unless you use your abilities…and now we know she can be killed. We have hope."

"Which will be shot in a second if she captures one of us," I said. "She took my memories when she first came out of the vault. I had to use my Triune to stop Elijah levelling Warrington. She knows she failed to kill me in Thríbhís Mhór, and that I survived the Darklands."

"She would have found out eventually," Issac said.

It didn't make me feel any better, but it was what it was. "She'll be fortifying her position and gathering the Dark to her. There'll be an assault on the castle… and soon."

"Yes, I agree, but she won't be satisfied with simply taking Camelot from us," Greer said. "She'll make us suffer first. Revenge makes people do terrible things."

I lowered my gaze, the mountain we had to climb grew taller and taller with every passing moment.

"I don't even know how to use it," I said, "let alone how to get close to her."

"Ramona and I can study it," Issac offered. "See what properties it has. Perhaps that might shed some light."

"And some of our best commanders are on their way to Camelot as we speak," Greer added. "Our strategy will depend on what that flower is capable of."

Picking up the crystal, I held it in my palm for a moment, then offered it to Issac. "Take care of it."

He took it from me and nodded. "I'll protect it with my life." He rubbed his thumb over the surface of the crystal, smiled, then took his leave.

Greer rose and rounded the table, her Light simmering.

"You better get some rest," she murmured. "There are a lot of people who want to see you, your parents included, but I think they can wait until morning."

"If it's all the same to you, I'd like to stay with Elijah."

"Madeleine," Greer said, laying a gentle hand on my shoulder, "after what you've done for our people, you can do whatever you want."

5

I woke the next morning, my back stiff from sleeping on a hard mattress in the infirmary.

It was reassuring to know I wasn't immune to ordinary aches and pains, though a touch of Light saw it ease out of my muscles as I turned over.

Elijah sat in the bed next to mine, propped up by a pile of pillows, exactly where I'd last seen him—staring into nothingness.

The light in the infirmary was bright, but it was needed for the tiny hospital to work. Since the facility had been upgraded, a lot of extra beds and equipment had been rolled in. I'd noticed a laboratory had been set up in one of the rooms at the back, as well as a hybrid operating theatre—there were some injuries Light couldn't heal.

The curtains around the beds fluttered and Ramona slipped through. She held a tablet in her hands and a studious expression. Her auburn hair was pulled back in its usual severe braid, though a few strands had broken loose. She must have been up all night. It was good to see some things hadn't changed.

I sat up and rubbed my eyes, curious to see what her thoughts were on Elijah's condition.

"I hope I didn't wake you," she murmured. "I just wanted to check on Elijah."

"No, I tend to just wake up when I've had enough sleep these days. Not much disturbs me."

She perked up, her doctorly instincts kicking in. "Really?"

"I understand myself a lot more these days," I replied. "What about Elijah? Any change?"

"Understand what? Did you learn more about your Triune from Merlin?"

"Ramona," I said with a groan.

She clucked her tongue and waved me off. "Okay, okay, I'll interrogate you later." My bottom lip began to tremble and she rounded the bed. "Madeleine?"

"What if he doesn't wake up?" I whispered. "All over a silly mistake…"

"Mistake?"

"He used his Colours to kill that demon, not his arondight blade," I told her. "If I'd been paying more attention, I—"

"You can't blame yourself," she interrupted. "Elijah's strong. He's got eight hundred years of understanding under his belt. If anyone can work through this, it's him."

I hoped she was right. He'd given up his home and his people to come back to Earth with me, and the first thing that'd happened… He would argue he knew the risks, but I just wanted to protect him from all of this. Absorb the blow so he didn't have to take it.

I rubbed my arm where Elijah had woven his prism. Maybe I did understand love a little after all. Love was sacrifice.

I watched Ramona as she checked Elijah's vitals in the meticulous and methodical way she had—pulse, temperature, pupil response. She lifted his eyelids and put in some saline drops to prevent his eyeballs from drying out and finally tapped in the results on her tablet.

"Well, he's fit and healthy," she declared. "Everything that's going on with him is on a spiritual level. The two halves of him have disconnected and are running independently. The biological body is a complex factory—"

"Is she still talking about biology?" Issac asked, his voice filtering in from the other side of the curtain.

"You can come in," I drawled. "We're all decent."

He poked his head through the curtains. "Well, thank the Light for that."

"You don't seem concerned," I observed. "Neither of you."

"Druid psychology is different from ours," Issac replied. "What appears to be dire, isn't at all so terrible. Now that Elijah's Colours have come back, there seems to be a more spiritual quality to his being, though he'll always be vulnerable because of his time as a demon."

"I remember," I said. "His soul has some scarring

because of Ikakantor's shard. But what about the knot?"

"Well, that's the interesting part. His condition appears similar to a psychosis," Ramona explained. "It's a mental disorder where thought and emotions are so impaired that contact with reality is lost. In Elijah's case, his Colours came back so suddenly and with so much force, they caused a blockage, or *knot*, between his soul and his mind."

"Merlin was right," Issac said. "There's nothing we can do but let him work it out on his own."

"How can you tell?" I asked.

"I tried to connect with his mind," he replied. "I can't do it like you can, but I could just enough to see the disconnect."

Issac went into Elijah's mind? I knew how hard it must have been for him, considering our history. In the few occasions the two men had been alone with one another, they'd ended up in a series of spectacular fights. The first time was their punch up in the rainforest. The second was a sword fight in the middle of Camelot. Issac was into me, but I was into Elijah, but that was a whole other can of worms I hoped we'd worked through enough to put it behind us.

"I'm blocked from seeing his soul," Ramona added. "The power he unleashed must have been extraordinary. The knot is so bright, it's blocking everything else."

I glanced at Elijah. "So we just have to wait."

"It seems like it."

"By the way, I've been in the lab all night," Issac said, showing me the flower.

I raised my eyebrows. "Proof of life?"

"I haven't busted it open, if that's what you mean," he told me.

"What is that?" Ramona asked, staring at the crystal.

"A flower," I replied. "An *extremely secret* flower, FYI."

Her eyes widened slightly and she nodded. "A gift, I presume?"

I nodded. "From Ynys Wydryn itself."

Ramona stared at it, growing more perplexed as the seconds ticked by. "What does it do?" I dragged my finger across my throat and she gasped. "Really?"

"That's what I've been sitting in the lab trying to figure out," Issac replied. "How and why."

"It's a plant," Ramona mused. "Poison?"

"I wouldn't think it's that simple." He closed his hand around the crystal. "I'm keeping an open mind."

"Well, I know nothing about these things," I said as I pulled on my boots. "I'll leave the microscopes to you guys."

"Are you hungry?" Ramona asked. "I can get something sent in for you if you are."

"Elijah's locked in his mind," I said uneasily. "He won't know I'm here. This is his journey and he must take it alone." *As much as it grieved me.* "I think I need to show my face around Camelot. It's pretty dour out there."

Issac smiled as if he knew a secret I didn't. "That's a good idea."

"For some reason, I'm a beacon of hope." I shrugged and gestured to Issac's closed fist. "The real hero is suspended in quartz."

When I was ready, Issac walked me outside.

His usual put-together appearance was relaxed, his hair was messy but still artful, and his usual posh woollen overcoat was nowhere to be seen. He wore the same tactical gear and muddy boots as everyone else. There was even stubble on his jaw.

"What's with this?" I asked, rubbing my palm over his cheek. "Forget your razor?"

He jerked his head away. "*Madeleine.*"

"What?"

"I can't," he said, shoving his hands into his pockets. "It's…" *His heart still hurt.*

I wanted to apologise, but the words died in my throat. He had to stand there and watch Elijah and I be together, all the while trying to mend what I broke. No one could choose who they loved, and I wish I could have done something.

"We'll let you know if we find out anything," he said, filling the awkward silence. "Or if anything changes with…" He coughed and backed away.

I nodded, allowing him to make his exit into the infirmary as seamless as possible.

Sighing, I held onto a few stray tears and began to stroll through base camp. Above, the very tips of Camelot's towers scraped against low-lying cloud cover, making the ruined castle seem even more mysterious than usual.

Sometimes I wished I had just a drop of the wisdom Merlin had. Or a drop of a drop of the Lady of the Lake's. Maybe then I'd know what to say.

"Madeleine!"

I turned and saw Amanda cross the crumbled road, but I had to do a double take. Her usually mousy blonde hair was fiery red. Even in the gloomy winter light, it shone with a thousand strands of orange, red, and even flecks of yellow and purple. The way it flickered as she moved, I knew it had to be Light assisted.

"Amanda," I said, my encounter with Issac put on the back-burner. "*Your hair.*"

"I know," she said, twirling a lock around her finger. "I needed a change. With so much going on around here, I needed to feel the fire, if you know what I mean."

"Did you do that with Light?"

She nodded. "A little, but it turns out Maisy is a pro with a tube of dye and a bottle of peroxide."

I laughed, my heart swelling now that I was amongst friends. The whirlwind was still, if only for a moment.

"It's good to see you," I murmured. "You have no idea."

"Likewise! Camelot has been so tense ever since Morgana blew up the archive. Aiden is out of his mind with the damage."

"Speaking of Aiden…" I wiggled my eyebrows up

and down and Amanda's cheeks turned the same shade as her hair.

"Are you hungry?" she blurted out, awkwardly changing the subject. "The kitchen is open round the clock now. It's chicken schnitzel day."

I tilted my head to the side. "Schnitzel?"

"Crumbed chicken."

"Sure. I could do with some food. I'm feeling a little hangry." *As long as it wasn't venison with a side of lion,* I thought.

"Well, I'm not keen to see you hangry." Amanda threaded her arm through mine. "One hole in Camelot is enough."

"*Hey,*" I complained, "I'm not that dramatic."

Trent and Maisy were at our regular table when we walked into the newly prefabricated cafeteria. When I said 'regular table', I meant they were located in the general area it used to be in the draughty khaki tent.

They each gave me a hug while Amanda rushed to get us some food. I wasn't used to being waited on, but it was kind of nice to have friends looking out for me. I also liked that they didn't treat me as if I was the next best thing since Arondight and Excalibur. I didn't need that kind of pressure.

I was overly aware of all the eyes on us as Amanda slid into a chair and pushed a tray towards me. I took one of the plates and we set ourselves up with cutlery and salt and pepper.

"I know you can't tell us what you saw," Trent started, voicing what was on everyone's minds. "You know, what with Morgana being an epic mind reader and all, but can you give us any good news?"

"We made it back," I told him. "That's a step in the right direction."

"So, you saw the Druids?" Amanda asked, her eyes widening in awe. "What were they like?"

I chuckled and plucked a French fry from my plate. The kitchen was really moving up in the world if we had hot chips on the breakfast menu.

"C'mon," she complained. "I'm dying know."

"Yeah, Madeleine," Trent declared with a good-natured kick under the table. "Give us a little crumb."

I didn't see the harm, so I told them about Thríbhís Mhór and what life was like there. The Druid's simple life where they connected deeply with nature had a certain mystical charm that made me misty eyed just thinking about it.

Maisy coughed. "Speaking of Druids… How's Elijah? We heard he's in the infirmary."

I sighed and worried my bottom lip. "It's not an easy thing to explain. He's… Well, he's got some things to work out in his spirit."

"His Colours?" Trent asked.

I nodded. "They came back too fast."

"Whiplash," Amanda mused. "Naturals get it sometimes, too."

"That's one way of seeing it." I shrugged. "I've never heard of a Natural being overwhelmed by their Light, though."

"It's rare," she told me, "but it happens.

Happened to my uncle years ago…before I was born.”

“There’s a story there,” Trent said through a mouth full of chicken.

“Shut your gob when you eat,” Maisy cried, slapping him on the arm.

“Ow!” he complained, crumbs flying across the table. “*Way harsh.*”

I smirked, comforted by the notion some things would never change.

“Hey, Madeleine?” Amanda nudged me with her elbow. “Isn’t that your parents over there?”

I looked up to see my mother and father talking to an older Natural I didn’t recognise. Mum sensed my eyes on her and caught my eye, waving.

“I think I’m being summoned,” I said, pushing my plate towards Trent. His eyes widened and he dug enthusiastically into my half-eaten schnitzel. “I’ll see you guys later.”

My parents came to meet me half-way.

“We were looking for you,” Mum said. “Greer said you and Elijah arrived last night.”

“Sorry I didn’t come to see you,” I began, attempting to fend off the dressing down I was about to receive.

“Oh, don’t worry about that, sweetheart,” Dad exclaimed. “You both went through the wringer on your way back.”

Mum nodded. “We’re just glad you both made it in one piece.”

"Oh, sure… I guess…" Stunned, I could only mirror her nod.

"Would you like to go for a walk with us?" Mum asked, laying her hand on my arm. The gesture was oddly gentle for her and I didn't quite know what to make of it, other than realising they wanted to talk to me about something.

"Okay," I told them. "I want to check on Elijah later, though."

Outside, the air was crisp, but snow hadn't yet fallen. It was getting late in the year and I hoped the absence of ice wasn't an omen. Fire was my affinity through both my Dark and Druid Triunes…and it was also Morgana's favourite parlour trick.

We walked through the lower city, keeping to the designated paths the archaeological team had set out. Vast areas of Camelot still hadn't been explored, but with things the way they were, measures had been taken so the patrols wouldn't step on something important.

I knew Aiden and his team loved broken pottery, but I didn't see the allure. I'd uncovered a few intact cups in my early days in the city and discovering those was far more exciting. Of course, the discovery of the archive had put an end to digging up dirt…for the time being, at least.

"It's my first time here," Dad told me as we walked along the thoroughfare leading up to the castle. "It's quite impressive. I didn't realise it was so large."

"It's a whole city," Mum said, giving me an

amused look. "There were thousands of Naturals before the cataclysm and most of them lived here. Druids, too."

"It puts it into perspective," I mused. "Unlike reading about it in the Codex."

We fell into an uncomfortable silence. I turned and strolled along a side street, trailing my fingertips along the side of a stone building. It was difficult to tell what it used to be, but residential housing was at the top of the list.

"We've been talking with Issac," Dad said, making me stop. "He explained a few things to us."

"About your time working together," Mum added as I turned.

I narrowed my eyes. *Here we go…*

"He explained how your Triune works," Dad went on. "How it doesn't change who you are, even though your soul is fundamentally made up of three different people."

"I don't have a split personality," I grumbled.

He ignored me. "Human Convergence wasn't about spirituality. It was about power."

"We were seeing this completely wrong, Madeleine," Mum said. "Like Issac did before he worked with you. We didn't understand…"

"Your Triune is about merging abilities, not the actual souls they came from." Dad glanced at her and then back to me. "What we're trying to say is…"

"We're sorry," she finished for him. "We jumped to conclusions and didn't want to listen."

I stared at them, not sure I was hearing their

words correctly. I hadn't heard it so plainly before, about being a Triune. Their apology was a catalyst for something that shifted deep inside me—yet another thing I didn't understand.

I began to tingle, my emotions pulling at every string inside my body. What did I say now? *You're welcome? I accept? Could you please repeat that?*

"About you and Elijah," Dad added. "Your mother and I—"

I had the overwhelming urge to ugly cry, and I wasn't sure where it was coming from.

Mum frowned and reached for my hand. "Madeleine… Your arm…"

I looked down and saw the prism on my right arm glowing. "*Elijah.*"

I didn't hear what my parents said next. I took off down the street, a pulse of power propelling me to the infirmary.

6

———

Elijah was awake.

Light knew how I could feel it, but my spirit was alive with the knowledge that the man who'd left his prism on my arm was calling out for me.

I burst through the infirmary door, a whirlwind of Light, Colour, and Dark.

Elijah was sitting on his bed, his legs kicked over the side. Ramona was flashing a light into his eyes, much to his annoyance, but she was thwarting his attempts to swat her away with surprising accuracy.

At my abrupt appearance, they turned…along with everyone else in the infirmary.

Elijah's gaze met mine and I stormed over to his bedside, an unexpected rage surfacing and exploding over everything in my way.

"Why didn't you just use your arondight blade?" I demanded, torn between slapping him and kissing him stupid.

"I had an opportunity," he replied. "The ritual wasn't enough."

"Wasn't enough?" I shook my head, confused. "The Druids found your Colours and brought them back. How could that not be enough?"

"We're up against impossible odds and I… I crave what I lost, Madeleine. It's who I am. I needed it back." He needed it back? Of course, I knew he wanted those things, but… "Sometimes destiny needs a little outside interference."

I couldn't believe what I was hearing. "Wait a minute… You did this on purpose?"

The infirmary fell into a palpable silence. My eye twitched as my power flared, gathering into a bomb of my own.

Ramona clapped her hands together. *"Right. Everyone out! Take a break and come back when the fireworks die down."*

The lab assistants and doctors gathered their things and shuffled out of the building, glancing at Elijah and I as they passed. We could have left, but I was afraid I'd blow a hole in the roof if I moved an inch.

The door closed, and we were alone for the first time since I'd declared my love for him underneath the willow tree in Thríbhís Mhór. Unfortunately for Elijah, this wasn't going to end quite the same way.

"I made a choice, Madeleine," he said. "One that backfired, but I had to take it."

"I don't understand. You almost turned yourself into a mindless husk."

"I need my Colours," he said. "Without them, I can't help you. Without them, I'm a liability. Dead weight."

My mouth dropped open. "You pushed yourself on purpose?"

"I saw an opportunity and took it."

"*I can't believe you*," I hissed.

"Madeleine, you don't understand. For the first time in centuries, I feel whole again." He grasped my shoulders, his emerald eyes sparkling. "*I can touch my soul again.*"

"You risked everything," I spat, knocking his hands away. "You almost blew up an entire city!"

"That was something I didn't foresee," he said sheepishly. "I didn't think it would be so…violent."

"Violent?" I threw my hands into the air. "I had to use every part of my Triune to contain the explosion! I almost lost control!"

"And that's why I need my Colours!" Elijah exclaimed, his voice rising. "I'm no match without them."

"So because I'm more powerful than you are, you had to go and do something stupid to catch up with me. Is that it? Is the size of your proverbial manhood that important to you?"

"It isn't about what you have," he fired back. "It's about me, Madeleine. *Just me.*"

"Did you have to do it on the street like that? You could have used your arondight blade!"

"Madeleine, *stop*."

"I won't stop!" I shouted. "You were reckless!

What if you couldn't unravel that knot? You could have been trapped in your mind forever!"

"I was a shadow," he murmured, my anger rolling off his shoulders. "I was less than a man. Merlin…"

I froze, my skin pricking. "Merlin, *what?*"

"Before the ritual at Brioglóid henge, he gave me some guidance."

And I knew exactly what he'd said. It slapped me in the face like a sopping wet fish.

"*Sometimes destiny needs a little outside interference,*" I snapped. "He said that to me, but in true Druid fashion, he forgot to mention the specifics. Please don't tell me that's what I'm going to have to put up with now that you're one hundred percent *head in the clouds.*"

"I know Druids can be a little wishy-washy about things, but I'm not like that," he said. "I haven't lived among them for a long time. I'm more human than anything."

"I'm so pissed at you!" I pinched the bridge of my nose. "You can't just go around risking your life without giving me a heads-up."

"You don't mind me risking my life, though?"

"Of course I mind!" I shrieked. "*Why are men so daft?!*"

A loud cough echoed behind us and I turned to find Ramona glaring disapprovingly at us.

"Are you done arguing yet?" she asked, tapping her finger on her tablet like an unimpressed schoolteacher. "I like to maintain a sense of calmness in my infirmary. It promotes *healing.*"

My cheeks heated and I grimaced. "Sorry?"

Elijah took my hand. "Perhaps we should go for a walk."

"May I suggest your route take you to a secluded part of the city?" Ramona said with a sly smile. "Half of base camp knows your business. We don't want them to hear how this ends."

"Ramona!" I shrieked, the colour in my cheeks turning to flame.

Elijah pulled on my arm, taking advantage of my moment of stunned embarrassment to drag me from the infirmary.

Eyes followed us as we made our way through camp and into the lower city. In that moment, embarrassment was my middle name.

"One day, I'll tell you about the Camelot I knew," Elijah said as we strolled up the main thoroughfare leading to the castle.

"One day?"

He'd been sharing his body with a shard of Ikakantor for centuries and there were more gaps in his mind than memories, but his life as a Druid seemed as sharp to him as if it'd happened yesterday.

"There's a lot going on. It doesn't seem like the time for stories." He paused, his gaze raking over the courtyard.

I hadn't seen the archive since the day I'd faced Morgana, and the sight of it was jarring. Now that the melted rock had solidified, it reminded me of the remains of the hillside after I'd called up the lava to swallow Ikakantor's demon horde—an extinct caldera.

The hole in the roof was a jagged mess, as was the courtyard and the priceless Pendragon mosaics.

I stood at the edge and peered into the depths. I spotted Aiden inside, standing on one of the lower levels, guiding a load carried by a Light-assisted crane down into the bowels of the vault.

"The vault won't hold her anymore," Elijah said. "Not even if he repairs it."

"How can you be sure?"

"She won't fall for the same trick again. Besides, her powers have grown. This time, she's called the Dark to her."

I raised my eyebrows. "And she didn't the last time?"

He shook his head, keeping his explanation to himself. Even I knew it would be impossible to fool a Celestial once, let alone twice.

Leaving the Naturals to their work, we moved past the castle and back into the upper levels of the city.

Once we were alone and out of earshot, I climbed up onto a ruined wall and sat on the cold stone, dangling my boots over the edge. The temperature was irrelevant to supernaturals like us—a little power and it was like summer flowing through my veins.

I reached for Elijah's hand as he climbed up next to me but pulled away at the last second. He didn't need my help anymore. He had his Colours and could warm himself just fine, *thank you very much*.

"Madeleine, what's done is done," he said.

I snorted. It was so done, it wasn't even funny.

"Merlin believed I could do it and who am I to challenge his wisdom? He's like, two thousand years old."

My eyes widened. "Two thousand?"

"I don't know." Elijah shrugged. "I estimated from the length of his beard."

I had nothing to say, so instead, I looked out over Camelot.

"I'm sorry," he murmured. "I know you're angry with me, but—"

"Shut up," I interrupted. "You've already told me why…but did it have to be in the middle of a city while we were exposed to Morgana?"

"It wouldn't have worked any other way. I believed in you, Madeleine."

I squashed the urge to shout at him again and forced myself to see things from his perspective. "You'd do it again, wouldn't you?"

He lowered his gaze. "Yes."

I sighed. I was the pot calling the kettle black.

We needed to make a pact. Something that bound us together in an equal partnership, otherwise, he'd drive me mad. Maisy had told me all about makeup sex in great detail, but after what we'd done under that willow tree, I knew Elijah and I didn't need the fighting part.

"The prism you gave me…" I began. "It's more than a declaration of love, right?"

"Yes," he replied slowly. "It's a promise. Kind of like a human wedding ring."

I rubbed my palm over my arm. "Then why haven't you asked me to give you one? It hardly seems fair."

"They're not really something a woman gives to a man," he murmured.

"I don't care," I declared. "You should know by now that I make my own rules. We're equals, no matter what."

"If you give me a prism, it will bind us. It's not something that's done. Druids change their minds and fall out of love you know."

"That's so not the thing to say to a woman you've spent the best half of a day arguing with, FYI."

He snorted and ran his hand through his hair. "What can I say? I love digging my own hole."

"Dig a little deeper," I said, nudging him with my elbow.

"Challenge accepted, *against my will*." He smirked and took my hand in his. "Remember when I bound you to me?"

"When you found me in the cage inside Ben Nevis?" I raised my eyebrows. "That seems like years ago, not six or so months ago. I can't even remember."

Elijah nodded and drew circles on my palm with his fingertip. "It will be the same. We'll be connected, but in a much deeper way."

"Deeper, how?" I asked with a shiver.

"When either one of us activates the prism, we'll be able to feel one another and connect." I bit my bottom lip and leaned against him. He was warm, his body familiar. "But not just in a physical way. Spiritually, too."

"I love you, Elijah," I murmured. "I want this. I want to be as close to you as I can. I'm not afraid of my feelings anymore."

"You don't know how much it means to me to hear that," he whispered.

"We're connected, Elijah," I murmured. "After everything we've been through, we don't need a prism to tell us that, but it will sure come in handy, don't you think?"

"*Extremely* handy." His smile widened into a grin and I knew his thoughts were once again on the dirty side.

He kissed me and I melted into his touch, the anger I'd felt washing away. We had our moments, but didn't everyone? Relationships were work, especially when it came to Colour bombs.

"Madeleine…" Elijah murmured against my lips. "I'm not sure how it will work for you. You're a Triune, only part of you is Druid."

"But you'll feel the full effect?"

"Yes." He hesitated, then added, "If you do this, it will be forever. There's no taking it back."

Forever? "Now I'm understanding why women don't give them. I thought it was a sexism thing."

Elijah chuckled. "Not quite."

I jumped off the wall, landing lithely on the path below, and Elijah followed suit.

We faced one another and our gazes met. I felt electricity zip between us through the simple connection and knew I was doing the right thing. He was my soul mate.

The certainty I felt it with was startling.

"Which arm?" I asked, my throat thick with emotion. "Is there a preference?"

"The right," he whispered. "It's always the right."

I pushed up my sleeves and he did the same, mirroring my every move.

"Curl your hand around my wrist," he commanded.

My fingers grasped his skin, my palm flush against his pulse. He did the same, and as we connected, my prism flared. Blue lines crawled up my arm, the geometric pattern glowing in a thousand shades of blue and purple.

As if sensing my intent, my Druid Triune bubbled to the surface and grew. My hand began to glow, then I felt the prism rise within me.

Silver, red, and blue merged into one holographic strand and began to twist up Elijah's arm. Lines split and merged, weaving a complex pattern I couldn't keep up with. With every inch I felt our souls reach out to one another and connect.

I saw into his deepest soul and I knew he'd claimed back the life that was taken from him. He'd risked everything to be the man he thought I deserved. What did he see when he looked into mine? *Maybe one day he'd tell me that, too.*

The prism crawled all the way to his elbow before the lines stopped growing.

"This is a representation of what you feel for me,"

he murmured as the prism sank into his flesh before disappearing completely.

"Man, I'm really complicated."

"The prism is a living thing and will change with the both of us," he added. "It's complicated now, but it might not be in the future."

"I highly doubt it."

Elijah chuckled and pulled me close. "It's faint now, but in time, the bond with grow with us and become eternal."

I pressed my cheek against his chest. "You're such a soppy romantic."

"Shh," he murmured, stroking a hand through my hair. "You'll ruin my street cred."

7

I stood on the outer wall of Camelot and looked out over the Clee Hills, surveying the land around the city with unease.

A week had passed since Elijah and I had returned and things were quiet. The air was charged with an unstable energy, the Light barrier flickering as if it was reacting to an imminent threat…yet nothing came.

It was as if Morgana had disappeared, but I knew we'd never be that lucky.

Wind tugged at my hair and I scraped it away from my face. Something was building to the north—an oppression that called to my Dark Triune.

I sensed Issac walking along the wall and glanced at him. He was wearing his fancy wool overcoat with the collar flipped up. The wind tugged at his blond hair, tossing it to and fro.

"Hey," he said, standing next to me. "Restless?"

"Restless is an understatement." I scowled at the charred hillside. "Where is she?"

"Don't be so keen to fight her," Issac told me. "We need all the time we can get."

"But she's gathering her strength while we're faffing about."

He sighed and leaned against the wall. Holding out his hand, he squinted up at the overcast sky. "It's snowing." He smiled and showed me the flake he'd caught in his palm. The little sliver of ice turned to water almost instantly.

"It's the first snow I've seen of the season," I murmured. "It's late this year."

"A short, but fierce winter."

"What an omen."

The snow began to thicken, dusting the wall and our shoulders with a fine layer of power.

"Spooky," Issac said with a chuckle. "We best go inside."

"Did you want to talk to me about something?" I asked as we climbed back down to the ground level.

He glanced over his shoulder. "Yes, but let's get indoors first."

"Ah, so it's one of those 'need to know' moments?" I sighed as he steered me towards a small building near the edge of camp. "There's a lot of that going around."

"We're at war, Madeleine," Issac said as he opened the door. "We can't be too careful." *When he put it like that…*

"Five years was a good run," I quipped, stepping into the warmth.

We were in his private quarters. It was a step up from the tent where we used to meet for our training sessions—for one, it was less draughty. He'd make me sit on an uncomfortable pillow and meditate. For someone who was charged up through movement, trying to find the strength inside to sit still had been the ultimate challenge…more so than fighting demons.

There wasn't much to look at besides a bed, a set of chairs and camp table, a trunk, a laptop computer, and a pile of papers. A map of Shropshire was pinned onto a cork board that leaned against the wall. Various dots and highlights marked points and routes of interest, and the outline of Camelot was scrawled amongst the illusioned landscape.

"You've really come up in the world," I declared, looking around the room. My gaze fell onto a pair of familiar cushions and I wrinkled my nose. "Except for those awful things."

Issac laughed and sat on one of the folding chairs. "Don't disparage the cushions."

"You're so posh." I plonked down next to him and leaned an elbow on the table. "You've even got a mini fridge!"

"It's full of milk for my tea."

I leaned back in the chair and eyed him. I knew things were a little out of sync between us, but he seemed a little on edge. My thoughts immediately went to the flower.

"What's on your mind?" I asked. "I know you didn't ask me here for tea and biscuits."

Issac coughed and shucked off his coat. Was he buying time? That was so not an Issac thing to do.

"You know something about the flower, don't you?" I asked. "What is it?"

"I have my suspicions, but that's not it."

When he didn't elaborate, I scowled. "Which are?"

"The Celestials took on flesh and bone, but they were spirit before. The flower…"

I pursed my lips. He thought the flower was a manifestation of the Celestial's spirit, their connection to what they once were.

"Don't get too worked up about it," he said. "It's just one theory of many."

"How can I not?" I argued. "You just implied that to kill her, we might have to destroy her soul. That's not a small thing."

He raked his hand through his hair.

"That wasn't it, was it?"

"No, it's not that," he replied. "I've been… Well, I've been working with Elijah."

"You have?" *It was news to me.* "Why wouldn't you say something?"

Issac hesitated, then asked, "Elijah hasn't mentioned it?"

I shook my head. "No, he hasn't. I assumed he was going to see Ramona. She's so militant about her follow-up appointments, even I'm afraid of her."

This revelation seemed to rattle him, but it only played across his face for a split-second.

"It's nothing sinister," he said. "I wanted to make sure there was no residual side effects from his overload. It was quite the ordeal."

"He let you work with his spirit?" I couldn't believe what I was hearing. "And it didn't end up in a fistfight?"

Issac chuckled and ran his hand through his hair. "We're both grown adults, Madeleine. We can work through our issues."

I grimaced and lowered my gaze. The 'issue' was currently sitting beside him.

"The reason I wanted to talk to you was… Well," he went on, "he's doing some odd Druid-related things. I can't be sure if it's normal or not."

My expression fell. "What's he doing?"

"He's carving runes into his arms with a crystal knife."

I could see why he was worried. To outsiders, it looked like self-harm, and after Elijah almost blasted himself into a vegetative state, Issac was right to be concerned.

"It's a nwyfre stele," I said, my brow furrowing. "Eliorla had scars on her arms, too. Fine lines that looked like runes. They were so pale, I wasn't sure if they were scars or tattoos."

"Eliorla?"

"His sister."

He looked surprised. "He has a sister? After all this time?"

"Druids live a long time," I replied absently.

Elijah had told Eliorla off for marking herself in the same way, so why was he doing the same thing? I was one-third Druid, but I didn't understand, and I probably never would. I'd only inherited Philomena's Colours, not her identity or memories—I still had to learn everything the old-fashioned way.

"Eliorla was the leader of the *neach-gleidhidh*—the guardians," I added. "They patrolled the Druid borders in the Darklands. I assumed the runes helped with that, but I never got to ask her."

Issac didn't say anything, which was out of character for a guy who liked to talk about his research in detail. I looked at him and knew something was on his mind. He had an epic brow furrow going on.

"What is it?" I asked. "There's something worse than Elijah scarring himself?"

"I'm no expert on Druid physiology, but it feels as if something deeper has woken in him."

"Deeper? Like what?" I twisted a strand of my black hair around my finger. "More Colours?"

"I'm not sure." Issac's frown deepened as he puzzled over his thoughts. "I've studied spiritual Light and the souls of humans and Naturals for my entire life. I've even seen what yours is like, Madeleine." He shook his head. "Elijah's…"

"You're worried about him?" Pigs did fly. But if Issac was concerned, then it must be serious.

"It could be nothing, but with Morgana out there, we can't be too careful."

I tensed, not liking how he was hedging around the subject. "Well, spit it out."

"He's connected to something."

I heaved a sigh of relief. "Oh, that's me."

"I'm confused…"

Even though it was awkward, I explained the prism I'd given Elijah and how it bound us together in soul and spirit.

Issac's cheeks heated, but he shook his head. "It's a likely explanation, but I don't think it's that."

"Then what else could it be?"

"That's the whole point. I don't know." He shrugged. "When Elijah was freed from Ikakantor's control, it left behind small holes where the shard had fused with his soul. Now they're filled with Colour, but they're still open wounds."

"Wounds that can be manipulated," I mused, though we already knew this. Elijah would always be scarred from what he went through.

"Yes." Issac nodded.

"Do you think someone is manipulating him now?" I pressed my palm against my heart and gasped. "Do you think I'm doing it by accident?"

"That's why I wanted to talk to you. You're the closest to him, Madeleine. If he's open to manipulation, conscious or not, I'd rather you were aware of it."

I nodded, my thoughts growing and taking on a life of their own.

"Maybe that's why he's putting runes on himself," I mused. "To protect himself against

Morgana and close off the openings. I'll talk to him about it."

Issac sighed in frustration and I totally got it.

"You know what the Druids are like," I told him. "They're always involved in some kind of subliminal shenanigans. I didn't even know Elijah had been whispering with Merlin about forcing his Colours to come back. Though Merlin would have me believe that he told me straight up. I can hear him now. *I should have been more perceptive and listened to nature, then I would have known.* It's the journey not the destination. *Pfft.*"

"He sounds like someone I'd like to talk to," Issac said. "Though it can hardly be helpful when facing something life-changing."

"Merlin would never do anything that wasn't in the best interests of the Druids," I replied. "But he sure knows how to screw with people along the way."

"The Druids went through a great deal and they found their place in the universe."

"They did."

"I wonder what will happen to the Naturals after all of this," he mused. "If we manage to end Morgana's threat against us and the Druids, what then? All we've known is war. Even in the last five years since the Dark Night, we've still been fighting."

"Sometimes I think peace is beyond us," I mused.

"If we win, what will you do?"

"I've been so focused on right now, I haven't thought about what's next," I mused. "What about you? What do you want to do?"

"If there is an end to this, I'll go back to New York," he replied.

"New York?" I asked. "After everything that happened to you there?"

His entire family died at the New York Sanctum in the Dark Night attacks. He'd been the only one to survive, and after having his sister torn from his arms by demons and killed, my heart beat extra time. Issac had more strength than I'd ever know. I wouldn't be able to return to a place like that, not after so much had been taken.

"Even after that," he said with a nod. "It was my home long before the Dark Night. I studied at Harvard and worked at the Sanctum. I won't let the Dark take those memories from me. Besides, the Naturals there have struggles of their own and the Regula needs a new representative to oversee the American operations."

"And you're the best person for the job."

"It seems so. Greer has approved it, pending our outcome here and Wilder will, too."

Suddenly, I felt a pang of sadness strike my heart. A world where Issac was thousands of miles away seemed so alien after our adventures at Camelot.

"It's not like I'm dying," he said with a chuckle. "It's just an ocean, Madeleine."

"Just?" I scoffed and shook my head. Despite myself, I smiled. "Whatever makes you happy."

We stared one another for a long moment. It seemed that awkward, heavy silences were fast-becoming our thing.

"Thank you for talking to my parents," I said after a moment. "They seem to understand about my Triune now."

His lips quirked. "You're welcome."

"Have you seen much of them? I've barely glimpsed them, so I assume they've got their portal research up and running again."

"They have," he confirmed. "Now that they can study Camelot's illusions in person, they're like children high on sugar."

"I… I really appreciate you speaking with them, you know. Things weren't the best between us." I glanced at him before looking away just as quickly. "All of us."

"I know things are weird right now, but it doesn't mean I won't help you," he murmured. "It's just that I have to distance myself to reconcile my feelings. It's not personal."

"I know," I told him. "You don't have to explain yourself to me. I never meant to hurt you…"

Issac picked up a plastic container filled with assorted biscuits and offered them to me. "Enough about that. Do you want some tea?"

"How very English of you," I said, peeling off the lid and taking a custard cream.

"You can take the Englishman out of England, but you can never take the tea and biscuits from his blood."

8

When I saw Elijah half an hour later, I understood why Issac was worried about the Druid's behaviour.

I stood with Ramona in the infirmary, watching him carve runes into his arms with his nwyfre stele. A towel spotted with blood sat next to him on the bed and he picked it up and wiped at his skin periodically.

"He's been at it for hours," she whispered. "He says it's nothing to worry about, but I've never seen anything like it… He just cuts and it heals, leaving behind a thin white line. There isn't even any ink so you can hardly call it a tattoo. He hasn't even flinched."

They were permanent prisms.

"Let me talk to him," I murmured. "I doubt it's as alarming as everyone thinks."

She raised her eyebrows. "Good luck with that."

"I promise to take it outside if it turns into another argument."

"Thank you," she declared with a smirk before striding into her laboratory.

Looking at Elijah, I sighed. *Here we go again.*

Walking across the infirmary, I stood over him, watching as he cut a line across the back of his hand.

"Elijah, what are the runes for?"

"They're a mixture of runes and prisms," he replied without looking up. "Runes are simple marks of intent or meditation. Prisms are more complex."

"Yes, but *what are they for?*"

"They connect me with my Colours."

I frowned.

"They're not like our prisms," he added and glanced at me. "Ours are linked to our souls. These are just regular prisms." He said it like I was supposed to get his meaning.

"Oh. I *don't see.*"

He grunted, focusing on the rune on the back of his hand. It was quite beautiful, almost like a mashup between a Norse sigil and a Hindu mandala. The line he cut bled for a moment, then shone with subtle holographic light before it faded into a soft, white scar.

"I gave Eliorla such a hard time for doing this to herself I kind of feel like a hypocrite," he went on. "She was only manifesting her calling as a *neach-gleidhidh*. She needed everything she could in the Darklands."

"Then why did you?" I asked.

"It's extreme, even for a Druid of her standing. It means she's completely dedicated to her calling. Her faith is unwavering." He cut another line and held up the top of his hand to survey his work. It was perfectly straight. Elijah sure didn't need a ruler *or* a protractor.

"And is it the same for you?" I glanced at his arm, noticing that he hadn't marked himself where my prism lay.

"You said to me that you were reckless, did the opposite of what you say, and rush headfirst into danger," he said. "Now I'm telling you that I can be vague, stupid, and eccentric...but know that everything I do, I do because I love you."

"Everyone thinks you're a little insane," I murmured. "But when you explain it like that...."

"I know it looks completely mad, but I promise it helps...and doing it in here seemed more sterile."

I lifted his hand and traced my fingertips across the lines. I felt his Colours hum beneath my touch and realised what they were for. "They're anchors."

He nodded. "They only amplify what's already there. They're more ritualistic and a little old-fashioned than anything."

"That's why not many Druids have them? They're out of fashion?" I rolled my eyes.

Elijah laughed. "They were more common eight hundred years ago—some elders had their entire bodies covered—but times were tougher than. Peace changes a society, Madeleine. They don't need to be so aggressive about their Colours anymore. Think of human tribes and how they tattooed themselves...it's kind of like that."

"Do you realise you give such long winded explanations? You need a good editor."

"I'm almost done." He laughed and set down the stele. "I've got one more I want to do."

"Can it wait until later?" I narrowed my eyes. "We need to talk."

"*Uh oh*." He froze, his gaze meeting mine. "About?" He fluttered his eyelashes and I knew something was definitely up.

"Someone's connected to you," I told him. "Issac felt it."

He pulled a face and shrugged. "I'm connected to you. You put that prism there yourself."

"But it's not me."

"Who else could it be?"

Exactly. I thought back to our time in Thríbhís Mhór and the ritual to call back his Colours. He'd been gone the entire day doing secret Druid things and Merlin had been pulling his strings behind the scenes. That's what led to Elijah's Colour bomb, after all.

I gasped. "You're connected to Merlin, aren't you?"

Elijah grimaced "*Sort of…*"

"Sort of? But he closed off the homeland after we left. How can he speak to you here?"

"He's not here," he told me. "It's a failsafe. If we need the Druid's help, I can contact him."

It was also why Elijah had forced his Colours. Maybe the reasons he'd told me were true, but the main one was to be able to contact Merlin.

Everything was one big conspiracy with those people. *I should have seen this coming.*

I slapped Elijah on the back of the head, my palm connecting with a crack of energy.

"Ow!" he cried. "What was that for?"

"For keeping things from me."

"I had to," he hissed. "If Morgana found out, she'd take me and be able to get to Merlin."

"Forgive me if I don't believe you," I retorted. "Merlin isn't that stupid."

Elijah's grimace continued and I wondered if his face would stay like that if the wind changed. How unfortunate for him.

"I thought Issac was talking about *our* prisms," I exclaimed. "I had to explain it to him. Do you understand how awkward that was for me?"

"Imagine how awkward it was for me to let him probe my soul."

"*Don't be dirty.*" I sat on the bed and sighed. "Just give me a heads-up next time you think about cutting your arms open with a scary magical knife, okay? You gave Ramona a heart attack and Issac wanted to find you a padded cell."

Elijah narrowed his eyes and snorted. "I bet he did."

"Oh get over it."

"And you can get under it," he declared, throwing me back onto the bed.

"Elijah!" I squealed as he leaned over and kissed my neck.

"When do we get our own room? I'm tired of

sleeping in the infirmary. I asked, but they're all out of willow trees."

I laughed, my annoyance at the Druid forgotten in an instant.

I knew everything he did was for a reason, I just wished he was more open about it with me. Why was I only now realising that a relationship with a Druid was going to be as frustrating as it was exciting?

"That's a sound I like to hear," he murmured. "Can I show you my rune?"

"Which one?" I asked a split-second before I realised what he was *actually* talking about.

He wiggled his eyebrows. "You'll see."

All my doubts and worries came flooding back the moment I left the infirmary.

I wandered through base camp, my lack of assignment weighing heavily on my shoulders—along with the curious stares I kept accumulating.

Elijah was busy preparing his runes, Issac and Ramona were studying the flower, Greer was doing Regula things, Thompson was off coordinating the city defences with Trent and Maisy under his command, my parents were buried under a pile of portal research, and Aiden was hard at work in the archive with Amanda. Everyone had a place to be, except for me.

Passing into the lower city, I debated going to see

Aiden, but I paused as an overwhelming urge to see my mother and father pressed into my heart.

They'd set up a research station in a small prefabricated building at the edge of base camp. Someone'd had the good foresight to put them between storage facilities, so it was quiet when I approached. *Must be an exclusion zone in case of explosions,* I thought wryly.

I knocked on the door before I lost my nerve. Dad appeared a few moments after a muffled crash, his hair dishevelled.

"Madeleine!" he exclaimed. "What are you doing here? It's good to see you. Come in." It all came out in one long run-on sentence, his enthusiasm leaving me spinning. "Bethany! Madeleine is here!"

The little building was packed full of equipment. My parents had lost no time in wrangling everything they needed to set up their experiments again, but I wasn't surprised after Edinburgh.

"Have you discovered anything new?" I asked, studying the piles of books, journals, and crystals littered over the table.

Dad grinned and reached into thin air. His hand disappeared and a moment later, he came back with a cluster of quartz crystals in his palm. The air shimmered, revealing a stool in the centre of the room.

I raised my eyebrows, wondering if I was meant to be impressed.

"Please, hold the applause," he declared dryly.

"It's a cloak..." I said hesitantly. It wasn't exactly

anything new. We used them every day, especially while hunting demons who hid amongst humans.

"Yes, but this one is different," Dad said, holding up the quartz. "We use cloaks and wards already, but this one is crystal-powered. Elijah mentioned the Druids used crystals for all kinds of applications, so we've been working them into our research."

"Naturals power everything with our Light," Mum added, appearing from where she'd been lurking behind a whiteboard. "There's always a draw happening, whether it's from a cloak or something as simple as warming our blood. In a bind, having a battery pack could be useful."

"And hopefully undetectable to the Dark," Dad declared. It was obvious he'd been dying to deliver the punchline ever since I arrived.

"Can you imagine the technological applications for something like this?" Mum gushed. "Clean energy! Too bad we're not about to disclose our existence to the human race."

For once I had to agree with her. Anything that was clean and cost-effective seemed like a good thing to me.

"Crystals aren't a new thing, though," I said.

"Well, no, but we've never been able to use crystals to store energy," he told me. "We only used them as amplifiers. The Druids worked out how to do a lot more with humble quartz."

"Their Colours work differently than our Light, though," I said. "Maybe Light can't be stored no matter what we do."

"That's what we're trying to figure out. If there's a way, we'll find it."

"What's it got to do with portals?" I wondered. "Or Camelot's illusions?"

"More than you think, actually," Dad replied. "Wards keep things out and Camelot's illusions, like the ones at the Sanctums, are called barriers for a reason. They reflect light…but what if we could use the composition of quartz crystal to reflect that light in on itself?"

"Sometimes I wonder if I was adopted," I said. "This is going straight over my head."

Dad chuckled and patted me on the shoulder. "We're trying to use portals and illusions to create a crystal Light battery."

"*Oh…*"

"Darling, you'll make her brain explode," Mum told him. "Don't worry, Madeleine. The science program at that academy was severely lacking. A strongly worded letter to Headmaster Islington is in order."

"Maybe he'll ask you to be a professor," I mused.

Dad snorted, earning himself a sharp glare from my mother.

"Would you like a cup of tea?" she asked, guiding me away from my father. "I sense we need some girl chat."

"Girl chat?" I stared at her, wondering when she went mad. Was it before or after I was born?

She clucked her tongue and practically pushed me to the back of the building where they'd set up a little living area. It was only three metres away from where Dad sat grumbling to himself, and I wondered how secret Mum thought this 'girl chat' was meant to be.

"You seem distracted," she said while she fussed over an electric kettle. "Oolong or Darjeeling? Wait… what am I saying? You're an Earl Grey kind of person."

"I am?" I didn't really drink a lot of tea, so I couldn't say. I didn't even know what the difference was.

"Earl Grey is good for the nerves." I didn't know if that was true, but I saw a theme emerging.

"I'm worried," I told her, picking up a sliver of clear quartz as the kettle bubbled. The place was littered with remnants of their experiments. "Don't you think it's been too quiet? After all the fuss Morgana made in Edinburgh…just to disappear? It's strange." I turned the crystal point over in my hand as she poured water through a strainer full of loose Earl Grey tea leaves. "And to not have any sightings? *What is she up to…?*"

Mum's expression faded and she took the crystal from me and replaced it with a steaming teacup. "All we can do is prepare. You and Elijah returned with hope, sweetheart. We're all in the same position. It's the not knowing that gets to us the most." She nodded at the cup. "Drink up, darling."

She was right, but my anxiety was getting the better of me. The more I dwelled on it, I wondered if it was my Dark Triune warring with the other parts of me. The dream I had about the Lady of the Lake seemed to confirm my suspicions.

I stared at my cup of tea, focusing on a stray tea leaf swirling around in the whirlpool created by my spoon.

We didn't have enough information to be proactive, so the most logical choice was to hold our position and protect Camelot. The problem was, that was what Morgana probably hoped we would do.

I thought about Edinburgh and the chaos Morgana had caused there. The same was coming for us, only tenfold. If we were in the one spot at the same time, she could just carve the city right out and squash us all.

Abruptly, I thought about something Mum had said about Camelot back at the safe house. *It's no Avalon, but it just might be the next best thing.*

Avalon… The Lady of the Lake hadn't said it, but I assumed because of the flowers and the Celestial's presence, Morgana couldn't walk there.

"What if we made Camelot like Avalon?" I blurted.

Mum blinked, surprised at my about-face. "How?"

"Camelot's illusions are unique, right? If a human walks towards the city, they just appear on the other side like nothing is even here. Space and time is folded so only supernaturals can enter. Would there be a way to sever it from Earth entirely? Scarlett said that's how Avalon was created."

"Perhaps, but the power used here is past our

understanding. We're trying to unravel it, but it's not a simple equation by any means…"

"Then we plant that flower and grow it all over and—"

"Madeleine." My mother took the teacup from my trembling hands and grasped my shoulders, forcing me to look at her. "No matter what we do, we have to kill her. Holding our ground is one thing, but it won't matter if she tears the planet out from underneath us. That means billions of innocent lives will be gone in an instant. Even if we could sever Camelot from this reality, would it be worth all of that?"

My bottom lip trembled and tears of frustration filled my eyes. "I just… I don't know what to do. Everyone is looking to me for answers, but I feel like all I came back with were riddles and a flower. *A flower.*"

She wound her arms around me and held me close. I breathed deeply, inhaling the scent of her vanilla perfume. She always smelled like sweet spices, even when I was a girl. It reminded me of troubled times growing up, and the scarce few times I got to see her past the age of six, but now she was my mother again. The mother I wanted all along.

"I've lost my way, Mum. I—" I sucked in a shaky breath to stop myself from sobbing.

"I wish I had the answers," she whispered. "It's my job as a mother to battle the monsters under my daughter's bed so she doesn't have to. I wish I could just turn on the light and chase away all the shadows…"

Pulling back, I sniffed and straightened my hair.

"One day at a time, sweetheart," she murmured. "One day at a time."

9

Ramona summoned Elijah and I to the infirmary the following day.

Hopeful she and Issac had found out something about the flower the Lady of the Lake had given me, we wasted no time hustling ourselves into the laboratory.

They were both bleary-eyed and tired but brightened when they saw Elijah and me. I knew the both of them had hardly left the infirmary since we'd arrived—their number one priority figuring out exactly what the Lady of the Lake had entrusted to us.

The crystal was suspended over a stainless-steel table, held aloft by fine metal clamps. Spotlights shone down on it, clear light illuminating the small, white flower within the quartz.

"It looks so innocent," I mused, staring at the bloom.

"It's made up of a compound we've never seen

before," Ramona said, her excitement palpable. "It's quite extraordinary."

"It's not quite biological," Issac elaborated. "There's a sentient quality to it, but not to the point of intelligence."

"Sentient?" I asked, raising my eyebrows. "Like it's *alive*, alive?"

"Yes and no." He sighed, clearly confused by their findings as well. "It's difficult to explain."

"The flowers grow where the Celestials walk," Elijah said. "They're a manifestation of the pieces they left behind when they took on flesh and bone."

"Yes!" Ramona exclaimed. "That's exactly it!"

"That's why Morgana's connection with the relic was weakened when it ran across the field," I murmured. "But how does that lead to killing her?"

"Celestials are ascendant beings," Issac began. "They exist on a higher plane, one far out of our reach."

"A higher plane?"

"They don't need physical bodies to exist. They are pure energy, similar to what we perceive as spirits."

"Ether," Ramona added. "Time and space don't matter to them, nor do the comings and goings of creatures like us."

"Not until some of them decided to slum it in physical bodies," I drawled. "That's where the trouble began."

"Temptation of the body is a story as old as time," Elijah declared.

Issac glared at the Druid. "The flower is their link to the past."

"A loophole," Ramona added. "Everything in nature has one. It's the universe's way of keeping the balance. Nothing can be absolute or truly immortal, not even Morgana."

"She'd like us to think differently," I drawled. "Immortal or not, the more powerful she becomes, the less chance we have to end this war before it comes to all out violence."

"That's our next step, Madeleine," Ramona told me. "Figuring out how to use the Lady of the Lake's gift to put an end to Earth's next mass extinction."

When she put it like that, the gravity of what we were facing caused a pool of dread to collect in the pit of my stomach. After obliterating us—and humanity falling as collateral damage—Morgana would move onto the Druids, then who knew how many other worlds in her search for true immortality. She'd grow in power, become even more unstable, and devour everything in her path. She was the One all over again, but this time, it was amplified a trillion-fold.

"How can we weaponise a flower?" I wondered. "Poison?"

"Well, Elijah's Colour bomb gave me an idea," Issac replied.

"Glad to be of service," the Druid quipped.

Issac ignored him. "I think I can gather the energies inside the flower to create a combustible detonation."

I blinked, his scientific ramblings suddenly made

sense. "You want to create a Celestial killing soul bomb?"

"*Cool*," Elijah declared, earning himself a sharp elbow in the gut from me.

"It wouldn't be without risks," Issac explained. "For one, we'd have to work out a way to contain the blast so it only envelops Morgana. Anyone caught inside the radius would likely suffer the same fate."

I sighed, knowing exactly where this was going. "I have to be the one to deliver it, don't I?"

"You got in and out of Camelot several times without being seen or tripping alarms," Issac said. "If we work on that ability, then maybe we can get you close enough to detonate the explosive and your Triune could contain the blast."

"I can nullify Light and Dark so I can become invisible, but it doesn't always work," I argued. "I doubt I could get away with it with a Celestial, and I haven't tried it with Colour."

"Ah, but you have…" Ramona said, "with Elijah."

"Please don't bring up my knot again," the Druid said. "She's still angry with me about that."

I shot him an annoyed glare. "I always assumed I could do those things because of my Triune. When the abilities mix together, they sometimes cancel each other out, but only when I put my mind to it." I grimaced. "I don't always remember…like on the train. I could've made sure we weren't seen by anybody, but I was too focused on Morgana to think about demons."

"It *straightened* out in the end," Elijah quipped.

"Luckily for you," I fired back.

"Point is," Ramona declared in an attempt to stop another argument from breaking out, "is that your Triune allows you to create a unique barrier of your own. Essentially, it's just a cloak, but when you put your mind to it, you can contain all our supernatural abilities."

"I'm not a superhero," I grumbled. "What if it doesn't work?"

"Then everyone in the blast zone will have their soul destroyed," Issac murmured.

"And how big is the blast radius?"

"The Lady gave you a single flower for a reason," Ramona said, gazing at the crystal. "It's potent."

"So big," I said, the dread rising in my gut. "*Really big.*"

Elijah laid his hand on my shoulder.

"Why me?" I asked with a sigh. "The Lady of the Lake granted a piece of her power to create the Light, and Morgana did the same for the Dark. Yet I can't use either part of my soul to influence their power directly. The Druids are completely separate."

"Because you're not a Celestial," Issac told me, "and neither are we. We are a completely different race of beings."

"Then how am I going to contain the blast from the flower? It's an extension of a Celestial's soul. I'm not in any way like them."

Issac smiled and shook his head. "We're all an extension of a Celestial, Madeleine."

"The Lady of the Lake gave you the flower for a reason," Ramona added. "We believe this is why."

Our little group fell into a heavy silence, the weight of Issac's plan a burden none of us were ready to face. Of all the scenarios I'd imagined, this was one that had never crossed my mind.

"How long will it take?" I asked, staring at the flower.

"Soon," Ramona replied. "We just have to hold on a little while longer."

"So much is riding on me," I whispered. "What if I fail?"

Elijah wrapped his arm around my waist. "We can't let what if's rule our hearts. It's a lot, but we do the things we must in order to protect our world. You told me that, remember?"

I nodded. "It's me between the end of everything. An accident created me and now…"

"I'm beginning to believe it wasn't a mistake," Ramona said gently. "Fate rarely makes herself known until the last possible moment, or at least our understanding of it."

I wondered what Scarlett would make of that and all of this. If she and Wilder ever woke from their comas, they'd be in for a shock or ten. The last Celestials who could cross into our world, the Lady of the Lake and Morgana.

"Sometimes I don't understand how I do things or why I act the way I do," I told them. "Light wars against Dark, and it's the same inside me. I was at peace in the

Druid homeland… I wonder why that was?” I shook my head, clearing the turmoil in my words. “Sometimes the Druid part of me feels like it’s completely absent here. Maybe it is completely environmental.”

“I wonder how it’ll be affected when or if the Dark is completely eradicated from Earth,” Ramona mused.

“Logic assumes that its influence will become dormant,” Issac said, looking at me. “Just like you feel with your Druid Triune.”

“You’ll likely still be able to use all your abilities,” Ramona added. “Just like you can still use your Druidic Colours.”

I grunted, lost in thought. Somehow, I had a feeling there was more to come and I wouldn’t know what any of it meant until the world stood on the brink of annihilation.

Issac glanced at Elijah. “We’re going to keep working on it.”

“Let’s go outside,” the Druid said loudly. “It feels like snow. I know how much you like snow, Madeleine.”

“I don’t—”

He grabbed my arm and steered me out of the laboratory, through the infirmary, and out the door.

“Subtle,” I drawled.

“You were getting all crackly,” he told me. “Didn’t you feel it?”

I shook my head. “I didn’t feel anything.”

“You get that strange eye thing.” He took on a

thoughtful look. "Interesting…you never got it on Thríbhís Mhór, even when fighting the relic."

"It's those damn demons," I drawled. "Imagine if I was just Light and Colour."

"Then you'd be a glitter angel!"

"You didn't just say that to me."

He grinned. "Seems like I did!"

I shook my head and moved away from the infirmary. The sky was heavy with cloud cover, but there was no snow, just muddy slush.

The Lady of the Lake had told me so many things when I met her in Avalon, though much of it was riddles and truths mixed with memory. *When the time comes, all will be revealed.*

"What are you thinking about?" Elijah asked, standing beside me.

"The Lady and the things she told me," I replied. "Her story was so sad. Her people craved a different life and it destroyed them."

"I suppose they devolved in order to make themselves flesh," he mused. "Issac said they were considered ascendant beings. All civilisations are developing towards enlightenment."

I looked up at him. "Enlightenment?"

"It's like evolution, I suppose. There are people who believe intelligence will evolve to such an advanced point that consciousness will transcend the body."

"And will ascend," I murmured.

Elijah nodded as another flutter of snow began to

fall around us. I wondered how he knew it was coming?

"She said there's a third Celestial," I said, catching a flake of snow in my palm. It melted almost instantly, and I rubbed my palm on my trousers.

"A third?"

"The Lady implied she was good, but a victim of her circumstances…and that she's trapped in another reality." I looked towards the sky. "I wonder what she's like."

"That's a story forever beyond our knowing, I suppose."

I began to fidget, the revelations we'd just learned tumbled around in my mind. They were creating a static charge of unstable energy that would blow up in my face if I didn't do something to dispel it.

"I'm going to train for a while. I'm too worked up to focus on much." I drew in a deep breath, the cold air invigorating. "Meet me for dinner?"

Elijah nodded and kissed me on the lips. "Your father asked me to help with his crystals."

"He did?"

"I'm collecting parent approval points," he replied.

"Oh. Good."

"Don't worry," he murmured. "I have a tingly feeling that things are on the right path."

I paused, something unspoken hovered between us, before I began to walk towards the training yard.

"Madeleine?"

I turned and our gazes caught. He looked so handsome and powerful standing in the middle of the muddy camp, his pitch-black tactical uniform somehow alive with the holographic spikes of Colour he'd awoken.

"I love you," he said, his lips pulling up at one side.

I smiled and wrapped my hand around my right wrist, feeling my prism warm. "I love you, too."

10

Later that afternoon, I was in the practice yard with Maisy when Greer summoned me.

The thought of news was equal parts relieving and concerning. Things had been too quiet, especially after Morgana's explosive entrance…or was it an exit?

The vault was still in ruins, but the archive's roof had been mostly repaired. The snow had caused work to slow, but the Naturals had magical ways of pushing through the adverse weather.

I left Maisy behind—exhausted, dripping sweat, and cursing my name—and made my way to the command post in the centre of base camp.

"Hey, Madeleine!" Aiden fell into step beside me. His wild hair blew in the wind, becoming even more tangled than usual.

"Hey yourself," I replied.

"I've hardly seen you since you got back," he said. "I'm glad you're okay."

"Thanks. It was a wild ride."

"Were you summoned too?" When I nodded, he added, "I wonder what it's about?"

"The thorn in our ~~arse~~ cheek, I suppose," I drawled. "Hopefully, it's good news. It's three weeks until Christmas."

Naturals didn't really celebrate Christmas—it was a human thing—but some traditions had crept into our day to day lives over the centuries. The kitchens in the Sanctums put on a special lunch and some people gave gifts, but we never really decorated.

Jackson and Esme issued a Christmas challenge in London every year that saw sparkly tinsel wrapped around the Lady of the Lake statue in the foyer— much to Greer's displeasure. To their credit, they did hang a suitably themed, glittery, purple and gold star from her marble sword—the sword being the first incarnation of Arondight.

"So…" I glanced at Aiden, "you and Amanda, huh?"

He coughed in an attempt to cover his reddening cheeks.

"You broke every female heart on the archaeological team," I added. "Including a few male ones as well."

He rolled his eyes and straightened the collar on his jacket. "Hardly."

I shook my head. He still had no idea how magnetising he could be when he set his mind to it. If I asked the female population of Camelot, they'd add how he *didn't* have to try. He was Aiden Thompson, the hottest Natural on the nerd scale.

"How's Elijah? Recovered from his Colour adventure?"

"Adventure?" I snorted. "Is that what we're calling it now?"

"I wasn't sure how to mention it without it sounding bad."

I sighed. "He's okay, I guess. He's taking his reclaimed Druid status startlingly serious."

"Ah, Ramona told me about the runes. In all the research I've done over the years, I hadn't heard about it before."

"I'd like to say that he'd gladly tell you all about it after this is over, but Druids are rather secretive…and vague."

"Extremely vague," Aiden said with a chuckle.

The weather had turned again before we reached the command post. Aiden held the door open for me, and we moved into the warmth.

Elijah was perched on the table and when he saw me, he blew a kiss in my direction.

"You were invited?" I teased.

"I'm important now. *Fancy that.*" He was the only available representative of the Druids, and all things considered, he was the next best thing to the Druid advisors of old Camelot. Then there was the part where we'd gone to Thríbhís Mhór together.

It seemed everyone who was anyone at Camelot was in attendance. The old crew was back together again, signalling this wasn't any old meeting.

Greer was the protector of the Codex—the closest thing that Naturals had to a spiritual leader—and the current acting Inquisitor of the Regula.

Issac was Greer's second-in-command and currently eyeballs deep in Celestial killing flower research.

Next was Caleb Thompson, Aiden's older brother. He was head of security at Camelot. I always knew him as Thompson, so calling him by his first name was strange.

Aiden was a bit of a wild card with his archaeological presence in the city, but he was the best historian the Naturals had. As he'd always taught me in history class, the hardest fought lessons of the past can guide us into a brighter future.

I was in attendance because of my Triune and the advantages it had brought me…and the path it had set me on. I still didn't feel like the equal of anyone in the room and missed Scarlett and Wilder keenly in moments like these.

"Thank you for coming," Greer said as we sat around the table.

Elijah nudged me under the table with his boot and I resisted the urge to pinch him. He'd become so fidgety since his Colours came back—even more than usual.

"We've been receiving reports that demon activity is increasing around the world," she continued. "All Sanctums have seen a significant increase in exorcisms and skirmishes. It's not at the rate we dealt with during the war, but enough to notice an upward trend."

"I assume this will hamper our operation at Camelot?" Issac asked.

"At this stage, the extra reinforcements the Regula requested have been ordered to stay where they are," she went on. "We're spread thin as it is but leaving holes in our overseas operations is not acceptable."

"Morgana's pulling our focus away from Camelot," I argued. "She's trying to divide our forces."

"There's no need for her to do such a thing," Aiden mused. "Morgana could strike us down whenever she wanted."

"She's playing with us," I declared. "She thinks that if we had something, we would have used it already. This is all just a game."

"I agree, but we can't stand by while people suffer," Issac said. "We have absolutely no information on where she is or where or how she will strike."

"Demon activity is one thing, but what *are* we doing about Morgana?" Thompson demanded. "We all know Madeleine and Elijah went to the Druid homeland, but no one's mentioned if they found anything that can help." He shot the Druid a piercing glare. "It was an awfully long way to go just to get his powers back."

"It's on a need to know basis," Greer told him. "You know we have to be careful, Caleb."

"Sometimes I wonder why I attend these

meetings, Greer. How am I to shore up Camelot's defences if I don't know what we're up against?"

"We do know what we're fighting, you know," I declared. "That isn't a secret."

"I remember the first day you arrived," he fired back. "How you've come up in the world."

"Don't be sore, brother," Aiden said with a sigh. "You have everything you need and more. You're head of security at Camelot! *Cam-e-lot*. Sheesh."

"But did you meet the Lady of the Lake?" Thompson asked. "Did she tell you how to kill Morgana? *Can* she be killed?"

"She gave us hope," Elijah said, speaking for the first time. "And where there's hope, there is Light."

"You know, this is frustrating, and I know what's going on," I quipped.

"You know, you say so little for someone who was a raging demon arsehole a few weeks ago," Thompson fired at him.

"The hole is still there," the Druid drawled. "Believe me, I checked."

"I know it's frustrating, Caleb," Issac said. "But we're still not sure what we have. We're working on it. When we're ready to strike, you'll be among the first to know. A battle is coming, and we need your help."

"No one knows Camelot as well as you do," Aiden said. "You've planned all the patrols, the defences, the trenches outside the walls…even the safe points inside the city. Even I couldn't do that and it's my literal job to dig up the place and find out how it works."

I glanced at Elijah, who winked. Thompson was such a drama queen.

"This fight is hard on everyone," I said. "Now we're going to be even more shorthanded. We'll have to compensate in other ways."

"We can't increase patrols," Thompson said, his lips thinning in displeasure. "The warriors are stretched thin as it is. Some teams haven't had an hour to themselves since the vault exploded."

"I want to ask your permission to return to your service," I told him. "You need help and me sitting idle isn't helping anyone."

Issac straightened in his chair. "But Morgana—"

"Might try and take me no matter where I am," I interrupted. "I will not hide behind the walls of Camelot when I can do *something*."

Thompson grunted, though I wasn't sure if he was impressed or annoyed at the prospect of having to deal with me again. My last tenure under his command was problematic at best.

"I'd also like to ask permission to join you," Elijah declared cheerfully. I glared at him and he shrugged. "Wallowing in the mud sounds like fun."

"I hope he's not being passive-aggressive because I'll throw him in the trenches myself," Thompson grumbled.

"He's being a Druid," I drawled, shooting Elijah a warning glare.

The Druid chuckled and leaned back in his chair, looking thoroughly pleased with himself. He only wanted to go because I'd put my hand up. He's become a bit clingy ever since I put that prism on him.

"I don't think it's such a good idea," Greer said. "I know we're lacking in resources, but without you and your Triune, we may not be able to get close to Morgana when the time comes."

"If Wilder was here, he'd probably say the same thing," I said. "But if Scarlett had her say, she'd be on the same page as me. I have the power to help, so why waste it? Life is a risk. None of us are immune."

"You have to follow orders," Thompson stated. "Just because you have extra powers doesn't mean you can assume your own command."

Greer glanced at Issac and he nodded.

"It would build morale," he said. "Madeleine and Elijah have become unlikely celebrities after they came back alive from the Darklands."

"Here's to survival!" Elijah exclaimed. "Hurrah!"

I rolled my eyes at the irony. Six months ago, I was treated like the enemy. I specifically remembered when an angry mob wanted to throw me back into the rift where the Dark had come from in the first place. I didn't like my matching Triune either, but it wasn't like I had a choice.

"Then who am I to argue?" Greer sighed. "Just keep to patrols in the immediate area. I'd like you to be close if we need you…" she gave Elijah a pointed look, "the both of you."

"Thanks, boss," Elijah said, giving her his best wink.

Her smile widened and I realised the usually

reserved Greer actually liked him. The more I thought about it, the more I realised everyone had been looking at him with a sense of bewildered enchantment. Elijah was slowly winning the hearts of Camelot.

"Don't get too cocky," I said, kicking him underneath the table. "The first thing you learn about being a Natural, is that this life is unpredictable."

He leaned on the table and battered his eyelashes at me. "Want to know what Druids learn?"

I deadpanned him. "Not really."

"Is this meeting adjourned yet?" Thompson asked, much to everyone's relief. "I've got a patrol route to assign."

Greer waved her hand. "Don't let me keep you longer than needed. I know you're all busy."

Elijah and I followed Thompson out of the command post, eager to see where he'd place us. All signs pointed to somewhere muddy and bleak as payback for the time when he arrested me and I escaped by nullifying his Light barrier.

Regardless, it was going to be good to get out there and contribute again, no matter the risk. I was a woman of action, and danger was my middle name.

"You do know that our prisms don't give us the right to be clingy," I muttered to Elijah. "We can be individuals."

"I *do* know that," he said loudly. "I just like being around you."

"What's gotten into you lately?"

"Ever since we returned to Earth and my Colours

rose, I have a sense of freedom I've never felt before. I can do anything, Madeleine. I'm…happy."

"Yeah, well, don't let it go to your head." I sighed and turned to face him. "I'm happy for you, Elijah, I really am."

He held up his arm. "I know."

I shook my head, bewildered. "It's just… I don't want us to think that this fight is in the bag just because we have the flower. We can still lose. *Badly*."

"We have hope," he told me. "And that is a powerful thing. Hope always wins in the face of terror and we never give into terrorism, even when it comes from a celestial being."

I smiled, his words lightening the load on my heart, and began to laugh. "I always think you're being an insensitive jerk, but then you come out with statements like that."

"You know, I've only seen Morgana once. It was when she'd just came out of the vault and she was stark naked, shooting fireballs out of her hands. I mean, everything was just out there. When you saw her in Edinburgh, was she still naked?"

"*Pervert*." I slapped him on the arm. "Of course, she had clothes on."

"The Lady?"

"*Celestials wear clothes*." I slapped him again. "Can we talk about something else now?"

"Is this going to be a thing with you two?" Thompson declared, turning around to glare at us. "Because it's already wearing thin."

"No, sir," Elijah said with a mock salute. "We wouldn't *dream* of making a mockery of your orders."

Thompson eyed him, then glanced at me.

"I apologise in advance," I said.

All the Natural could do was curse and shake his head. "Don't make me regret this, Greenbriar."

"You won't," I told him. "I promise."

11

Elijah and I patrolled the hills around Camelot for the next two days.

Nothing stirred, other than the wind and flurries of snow. The sky swirled with various shades of grey and not once did any blue poke through. Sometimes it felt like we stood at the edge of the world, but it was only the West Midlands.

My anxiety rose with every passing day without any demonic activity. It was a total cliché, but it truly felt like the calm before the storm.

We walked along a faint animal trail, following the tracks left behind by deer and other small creatures. A fox or two had passed recently, their footprints marking last night's snow and tracking over the rise, away from the city. Even though they couldn't see it, the animals knew Camelot was there and gave it a wide berth.

"Do the Druids celebrate Christmas?" I asked, my voice muffled by the layer of ice on the ground.

We'd been given white and grey trousers and jackets so we wouldn't stand out against the winter landscape in our usual black uniforms. I turned to see Elijah fussing with the zipper—it was stuck.

"In our own way," he replied, giving up. "It's Yule, or the winter solstice if you want to call it that. We have our own rituals that mark the passing of the heavens."

"So, no tinsel and presents?"

He laughed and shook his head. "Not really, but I'd ask the same for the Naturals. Modern Christmas is a human holiday."

"I wonder if the seasons are the same in Thríbhís Mhór."

"I never thought to ask."

I stared across the valley, watching Camelot shimmer in and out of focus. We were right on the edge of the city's illusions and as I tilted my head back and forth, it flickered like a hologram.

"What are you doing?" Elijah asked.

"The illusions," I replied. "They're thin here."

"Oh, I thought you were having a moment."

I shook my head and continued along the trail. "C'mon, let's keep going."

We'd walked another mile before I felt a change in the air.

Turning, I scanned the hillside, a chilling sense of déjà vu crawling down my spine.

"Something's out there," Elijah whispered.

My gaze flickered across the snow, knowing that holding our position was our best change—retreating wasn't an option. Camelot was too far away, and it would draw unwanted attention to the city. Besides, hiding behind the city's defences was a little cowardly for the Triune.

Movement drew my attention to the north.

Four greater demons inhabiting human constructs slunk across the snow, their feet gliding so lithely they hardly left any footprints in their wake. Darkness crawled all over them, oozing nauseous waves of power that called to my Dark Triune.

Four greater demons? It'd be a challenge, but nothing I couldn't handle. It'd be handy to know their true names… *Yeah, like they were going to tell us.* I'd kill them the same way I'd killed Ikakantor—by becoming pure Triune essence and tearing them apart.

They stood before us on the trail, their black eyes staring.

"Do you know who I am?" I declared, my hand curling around my arondight hilt. "You walk a dangerous path, coming here."

The demon who stood slightly ahead of the group —inhabiting its version of a human man—grumbled, "We know you, Madeleine Greenbriar."

"Then you know what will happen to you if you continue your mission."

"You are the one who doesn't understand." The demon's voice dripped with Darkness, the poison spreading across the hillside.

"Your mistress sent you on a suicide mission," I snarled. "I can kill greater demons."

His lip curled into a snarl. "Your ignorance will see the death of your world."

Elijah moved behind me, his breath quickening. What was I missing…? I reached out with my power, my Dark Triune begging to be unleashed to merge with…with the Darkness standing before us.

I gasped, the sound escaping my lips before I could stop it.

They weren't just greater demons… *They were Flames.*

The Dark was evolving. I'd said the same thing to Trent the day we'd been attacked outside Camelot, back when all of this first began. The Dark was evolving into something else, but I never thought it would be this. With Morgana's help, the Dark had become like us—like the Naturals.

I tensed and drew my arondight blade. Elijah and I hardly had a hope of standing against one Flame, let alone four. This was a fool's errand.

It was then that I realised why we hadn't seen Morgana since South Bridge—she couldn't exist in the same reality as her Flames. *She wasn't on Earth.*

Dread filled my heart and I tightened my grip on my sword.

Morgana suspected we were successful in our attempts to contact the Lady of the Lake, and now she'd scurried into her hole, setting forth her Flames to do her dirty work.

"*Madeleine.*" Elijah stepped in front of me. He could sense it, too.

"Four Flames," I murmured. *Four like the horsemen of the apocalypse.* "We can't hope to win…"

"We have no choice," he said, engaging his arondight blade. "We have to fight."

It was in that moment I realised I'd made a mistake by leaving Camelot. They'd been waiting for weeks.

"She wants me," I whispered, my breath vaporising on the air. "Morgana needs me for something."

"Struggling is futile," one of the demons rasped.

"Your fate is already sealed," another declared, raising a sword of his own.

"Surrender, Triune."

"Surrender and make this painless."

I glanced at Elijah. "I love you," I told him. "No matter what."

His emerald eyes glowed with heavenly blue. "Right back atchya, kid."

A sad smile pulled at my lips and I allowed my arondight blade to engage.

"So, you choose a path of pain," one of the demons called. "*So be it.*"

So be it.

I pirouetted, my blade arcing through the air. It collided with the demon's arm, a shower of sparks erupting as cold iron cut flesh.

Landing on one knee, I glanced over my shoulder and my breath caught. The demon turned, his eyes shining with crimson Flame, his body intact. *There wasn't a mark on him.*

The demon grinned and raised his arms. The rise of power pulled at my Dark Triune and I spun on my knee, pushing up as I faced my enemy.

A blast of Flame rushed towards my right and I threw up a web, deflecting the blow. A blade flashed to my left and I struck it with my sword, all while the demon before me laughed with malicious triumph.

We were never going to win, and he knew it. Our only chance now was escape, but could we lose them if we fled? We couldn't go back to Camelot, so where—

A portal.

"Elijah!" I shouted, reaching for my Colours. It didn't matter where we went, it just had to be away from here.

The Druid's blade collided with Flame, bouncing the energy towards the demon he fought. In that moment his gaze met mine and it was full of dread.

A wall of fire carved a path between us and I lunged. Elijah reached for me, our fingers desperately stretching towards one another, but it was too far.

"Madeleine!"

Crimson Flame spiralled, cutting me off from him. I cried out and flung myself at the barrier, but the fire buffeted me back, the heat searing my coat.

The circle shrank, the flames licking at my hair and scorching my exposed skin. I spun, looking for a way out, but there was none.

"Elijah!" I screamed. *"Elijah!"* If he heard me, I couldn't hear his reply.

I struggled in vain as the fire blocked out the sky,

my prison choking the air from my lungs. Gasping, I fell to my knees.

So, this was how it was going to end? Fire and brimstone? It seemed fitting for a Celestial like Morgana—red-hot anger the colour of flowing blood.

My heart ached for Elijah and the Naturals, but there was nothing else I could do. My fingers dug into the ground and molten rock burned my flesh.

Finally, the Flame swallowed me whole and darkness was all I knew.

I floated in nothingness, my soul beyond the reaches of Earth.

If this was death, it was awfully dull.

A pinprick of white sparked into existence and I stared at it, comprehension beyond me.

Maybe I was bound.

Maybe I was dead.

Or maybe in this place, it didn't matter.

The light gave me some sense of clarity and my thoughts were able to return. They tumbled into my mind like a tornado, twisting and turning, thrashing and tearing. I almost wish they'd stayed far away.

Where was I? What had Morgana's Flames done to me? Where was Elijah?

I reached for my arm, but I was without form and the motion did nothing. *Elijah…*

I couldn't feel him. Our connection was gone.

"Madeleine…"

The feminine voice drove me to sit, my soul forming a translucent body around itself. Perception was a strange thing when one was without form or feeling.

I wondered if this was what it was like being a Celestial. No. If that was true, ascending to a higher plane of existence wasn't that desirable. Somehow I didn't think it was supposed to be this boring.

A star shone in the blackness, growing brighter as it approached. The Lady of the Lake's ethereal body emerged from the glow, her hair flowing as if we were underwater and the current of time tugged at her silver strands.

"The Lady of the Lake," I murmured. In that moment I wondered if she had a name, and if she did, what it might be.

The Celestial knelt beside me and brushed her hand across my brow. "I have this short moment to speak to you then I fear you will be beyond my reach."

"Are you really here?" I wondered. "I saw you when we arrived back on Earth…but it I think it was just my own manifestation." She smiled but didn't answer. *So it was a little of column A and a little of column B.*

"Morgana will try to poison your soul," she murmured. "You must not let her twist your Dark Triune, Madeleine, for if she does…your world will be lost."

"I suspected it was that or she'd kill me," I replied. "It doesn't comfort me knowing it will be drawn out, but at least there'll be a chance of escape."

"Have faith, Madeleine," the Lady said. "You are stronger than you realise."

Even as she spoke, I felt a Dark presence bear down on me, pulling my soul away from her Light.

"You must warn Merlin," I pleaded. "He's connected to Elijah and if Morgana finds out, she could pass into Thríbhís Mhór."

"It has already been done. Caradhan severed the Druid's link before Morgana's creatures took you both." *Elijah was taken, too?*

"Where is he?" I cried. "Is he safe?"

"He lives…for now."

The Lady began to fade and I reached for her. My fingers passed through her hand and I choked back a sob. I'd let her and all of Camelot down.

"You trusted us to deliver the flower and end Morgana, and look at us…" I heaved in a shaky breath, tears of frustration clouding my eyes. "I've made such a mess of it."

"Hush, child," the Celestial murmured. "Your path remains true. Have faith…"

Darkness began to drag her away from me and her eyes widened. Wherever I was being taken, Morgana's influence was growing and pushing the Lady out.

"There are lies in her truth," she called. "But there are truths in her lies."

"That doesn't make any sense!"

The Lady grew smaller, floating on an invisible current. *"Remember who you are…"*

I reached out, my soul gasping for breath, but it was no use. Darkness took me and my thoughts were nothing.

12

———

My eyes slowly opened, the drip of water the only sound in the shadows.

I was in a cave. The stench of damp earth and mustiness filled my sinuses and I screwed up my nose to stop myself from sneezing.

After a moment, I raised my throbbing head and felt for my Light but found nothing.

My Triune was beyond my grasp and my abilities wouldn't manifest. Without Light to warm me, cold seeped into my bones and I shivered violently.

My coat was gone, as were my weapons, and my arondight blade was missing. The blade that'd chosen me, that'd been wielded by many Naturals throughout history, was likely gone for good this time.

My fingers scratched against damp grit and stone, finally curling around metal bars that drove deep into the rock.

It was a cage that reminded me of the one I'd been kept inside underneath Ben Nevis, the tallest peak in the British Isles. No Triune, no warmth, no light, no food…only Darkness.

I didn't even have Issac's spirit bomb, but even if I did, I was useless without my abilities. An uncontrolled explosion that could erase people was bad news. It was one thing becoming a martyr, but dragging innocents with me was unforgivable. I couldn't do it.

If this was a chess board, Morgana had me in checkmate.

An unexpected shuffling in the shadows made me scramble back, the abrupt sound alien without my supernatural senses to guide me.

A man edged out of the shadows, greyish light from an opening beyond illuminated his profile. It was a Demon-Flame, the one I'd struck with my arondight blade. Now I could see what humans saw, and I couldn't tell the difference between him and an innocent walking down the street. The starkness was shocking.

The demon chuckled, sensing my apprehension.

"You are not absolute," he told me. "We will rise once more, Triune."

"Am I supposed to reply to that? Because my care factor is zero."

The demon grinned at me. "She comes."

"Already? That's just great. Let's get out the good china, shall we?"

He laughed, the sound cutting off abruptly as he slumped to the ground. *Well, that was…creepy.*

I felt the Celestial approach long before she

showed her face. Her power was like a beacon, blazing in the nothingness of space and time, calling everything to it—a predator in a hostile land.

Finally, Morgana slunk out of the shadows, stalking like a lioness prowling across the wild savannah. She reminded me of a doll, delicate and beautiful, complete with a change of clothes.

Her long black hair fell in waves around her shoulders, her ivory skin glowed in the murky light. I didn't know where she'd found the time to go shopping, but I had to admit her fashion sense was impeccable. Heeled boots, black skinny jeans with trendy torn knees, a slouchy grey merle T-shirt, and topped off with a black leather motorcycle jacket. Total social media 'like' fodder.

I snorted. Morgana was definitely not breakable. She was a wolf dressed in sheep's clothing.

"Why capture me?" I asked, cutting to the chase. "You could have ordered your Flames to kill me and I wouldn't have been able to stand against them. Maybe one if I was lucky, but not four."

Morgana smiled and raked her gaze over me. "You're more useful to me alive than dead."

"I thought I was an abomination," I declared. "What changed? Do you like my attitude now?"

"Your attitude leaves a lot to be desired, but after I'm through with you…" Her smile widened.

Triune. What I'd become was what Wilder was afraid of all those months ago when he imprisoned me in Camelot. I was a weapon of mass destruction—

the key to raze the world to ashes…and the key to destroying her.

I could walk through Light barriers, render myself invisible to supernaturals, enter the Druid homeland, cast prisms, raise fire, and walk into the thin reality beyond life. I was Light, Colour, *and Darkness*.

Morgana was not absolute and she knew it. We were the fools in this story—we thought she was unstoppable and immortal. She was powerful, but she had an expiration date like the rest of us.

For Morgana, I was a coveted prize *and* the key to her survival, but only if I could be turned to the Dark.

"I won't help you," I snarled. "And I will die before you force me to Darkness."

"Oh, my darling, Madeleine. Before the end, you will choose to help me. I won't have to force you to do anything."

"I find that hard to believe."

"You are in the unique position where you can choose your destiny," she told me. "Three souls. Three choices."

"I chose life a long time ago," I snarled. "What someone is, is of no concern to me. I fight for life, truth, and goodness."

Her smile widened. "Life, truth, *and* goodness? Those are a lot of things, Madeleine. *Three* things, in fact. Perhaps we can begin with *truth*."

Life and goodness were interchangeable with Light and Colour, but truth…? Truth was a universal concept. I sensed a philosophical debate coming and I was tired already.

"And you think the Dark embodies truth?" I asked with a snort. "*C'mon.*"

"A hard truth lies within the Dark, for Darkness is death and in death, the mortal faces who they truly are."

I tilted my head. "How philosophical of you."

Morgana roared in frustration and beat her fists against the bars making them rattle.

"In all your violence and thirst for my blood, have you ever stopped to ask what I want?" she demanded. "Have you thought about why I was driven to madness? Do you truly believe I want to destroy the world I so wanted to be a part of?" Fire played across her skin, searing her clothes. "They convinced me to go with them and once we became flesh, *they abandoned me*. They left me behind, Madeleine Greenbriar, just like your people left you."

I stared at the Celestial, unsure what I could take at face value. Truth was hard won, especially in the midst of war.

I took a deep breath. "You weren't the same, so they shunned you."

"I didn't transition the same way," she went on. "Emotions overwhelmed my mind. Sensations burned my skin. I wasn't meant to be this creature."

I shook my head and scoffed, "It doesn't excuse you from killing innocents. Murder is an unforgivable sin, Morgana. Your disregard for life is abhorrent."

"I would have flourished," she exclaimed. "They made me this way. The fault lies with the Celestials."

Sighing, I rolled my eyes. "Sounds like an excuse to me."

"You do yourself no favours by driving the dagger deeper into my heart, Madeleine."

"What's the point?" I asked with a shake of my head. "What are you fighting for, Morgana? After you've destroyed everything, what then? Will it keep going on forever like your demons did after your imprisonment?"

"I will do as I please and not answer to you," she snarled.

The Celestial turned in a whirlwind of fire and flew from the cave, her light disappearing into the dark tunnel beyond.

"Where is Elijah?" I yelled after her. "*If you've hurt him…*"

But my cries fell on deaf ears. I was powerless here. All I could do was curl up inside my cage and wait.

Morgana would come back eventually, and the crazy would continue.

***

The shadows stretched into what seemed like forever.

At least I didn't have to wile away the hours on my own. The Demon-Flame hadn't bothered to get up, but I suspected it was because he was in a coma. Morgana was still prowling around someplace and her care factor towards her loyal servants was zero.

It was quite inconvenient—the demon's conversation skills were terrible, and his rotting meat suit was stinking up the place.

I fretted for Elijah, but no matter how hard I tried, the prism on my arm was dormant. I couldn't reach him for the first time in months and his absence tore a painful gash in my heart.

I curled up in the far corner of the cage, my energy at an all-time low. Being mortal sucked.

I was dozing when Morgana decided to grace me with her unpredictable presence.

"Oh great," I drawled, "another bedtime story."

"Are you cold?" the Celestial asked, peering into my cage. "You must be without your abilities."

"I'd ask for a blanket, but I already know the service here sucks. I'm going to give you one-star on *TripAdvisor*. I'd give you zero stars, but it's not an option."

"Being alone in the dark, severed from the world, isn't a nice feeling, is it?"

I snorted. "Oh, so this was a lesson? It wasn't slow torture?"

Morgana walked the length of the cage, the bars the only thing separating us. She stepped over her Demon-Flame like he was nothing, and continued until she reached one end, then turned and walked back.

"I was alone in the vastness of the universe, so I created my desire," she told me. "*The One*." Great. Story time was all about her blow-up doll. "Together we hunted the universe and its countless realties, searching for the Celestials who had wronged me. He was my tool, my companion, and my sword of retribution."

The One wasn't a sentient being, not like Wilder and Scarlett. The swords were vessels which allowed the Lady to remain on Earth, and that meant the One had been a shell all along.

He was a Flame without a soul.

Morgana was on a roll, not waiting to hear my thoughts as she continued her story. I doubted they mattered anyway.

"Sometimes I twisted their creations so they fought against them," she said. "I twisted the minds of their mortal worshippers. I set my demons into their peaceful paradises like a plague of death. I poisoned worlds and burned all that stood in my way. I've seen countless apocalypses and extinctions." Her eyes narrowed as ethereal fire played across her skin. "Even if they did not know it, I was their demise… each and every time."

"Until Camelot…"

"I've seen death, Madeleine, but I've also seen rebirth."

I narrowed my eyes. *Rebirth into what? How could anything grow from a smoking ruin of ash and terror?*

Morgana smiled. "Civilisations rise out of the ashes of those that came before. It is known in countless realities. The mortals spring back time and time again. They will do so again here."

"I won't allow it," I snarled. "Celestials should nurture life, not wipe it out on a whim so they can start again. Life isn't perfect."

"And how would you know what Celestials are meant for?" she demanded, her starlit fire sparking.

"The Lady of the Lake showed me a different way," I told her, jutting my chin out in defiance. "A way of benevolence and mercy, a way of *nurturing*."

"That *child?*" Morgana raged. "She'd slipped into their society so seamlessly that they didn't even know her truth." She began to pace, her anger rising. "She had them all fooled! *She still does*. The Naturals worship a *liar*." She whirled and grasped the bars of my cage, the metal glowing white-hot where her skin touched. "You would call that child a goddess? She was the instrument of your demise." Her lips curled into a vicious snarl. "When we walk into Avalon together, you will see her trickery and be glad I showed you the truth!"

My expression fell as I realised why I was sitting in a cage and not on the end of a sword.

"That's why you want me," I murmured. "I'm the only one who can get you into Avalon."

"You are the key, Madeleine. You still don't know the breadth of what your Triune soul can allow you to do. Your mortal flesh holds you back." She peered at me through the bars, her gaze stripping away my flesh until all I was, was spirit. "You alone, could transcend this place and walk amongst the stars...if you chose."

I pulled a face only a mother could love. "That's

the stupidest thing I've ever heard. My soul can't ascend."

Morgana's lips curled into a sly smile. "With my help, you could."

I rolled my eyes. Her tricks wouldn't work. I mightn't understand, but I wasn't stupid. Living a life as essence wasn't something I could comprehend, so why would I want it? Why would I leave Elijah to live as a spirit floating between worlds?

"Why can't you just go back?" I demanded. "Wouldn't that solve everything?"

"If only *life* were that simple."

"This is just a game to you, isn't it?"

Morgana's power flared, fire lightening the cave with a blast of heat. "This is about returning balance to the universe," she raged.

"Well then," I drawled, "it seems like I just pressed a button I wasn't supposed to."

It was all about spirits—or souls, whatever you wanted to call them. Essence and ascension. Power and revenge. Greed and guilt. Longing and contentment. Or in this case, meddling in affairs that were forbidden. The Celestials had dabbled in mortality when they weren't supposed to and now it had come to this.

I sighed and rested my head against the rock wall. Things were so much easier when it was just Light versus Dark.

"You're not making a good case for yourself," I mused. "If I take you literally, then you should be begging me to kill you. But first, you need to turn me so you can eradicate the Naturals, get into Avalon, kill the Lady of the Lake, then take out the Druids for helping the Naturals imprison you in Camelot's vault, then what? Have me kill you as the ultimate full stop? That can't be the end you've envisioned for yourself. It's pretty sucky if it is."

"How dare you!" She was fuming—steam was quite literally rising from her body. "I will not stand here and be rendered an imbecile by your flawed logic!"

I chuckled, the sight of her so angry was almost comical. "But logic escapes you, doesn't it, Morgana? You're broken, after all."

In a way, I felt sorry for her, but her path had led her to commit so many unforgivable atrocities, it was impossible to give her any benefit of the doubt. Morgana's intentions were evil, plain and simple.

I closed my eyes, exhausted. Ice crept back into my veins and I knew she'd stormed off someplace to throw her latest temper tantrum in private.

No matter where the Naturals or the Druids had come from, I would protect them until my dying breath. The Earth was my home, and the people and creatures who lived on it deserved the same courtesy. We were good. *I was good.*

And I would never fall to Morgana and the Darkness inside me.

Never.

I snorted and wrapped my arms around myself. That was all well and good, but I was still locked in a dirty, cold cage without my powers.

It was only after she'd left, and the shadows stole all time, that I realised why she couldn't leave her body and return to her people.

Ascension had to be earned…and Morgana hadn't earned a damn thing.

13

It was inevitable that Morgana came back.

Her presence no longer impressed me when she strode into the cave. I knew what she was now, and her starlight felt like a cesspool of evil—unlike the Lady of the Lake's pureness.

I forced myself to sit and sighed, wondering what nuggets of Celestial tragedy today's story time would bring.

"I'm so glad to see you're awake," Morgana declared with a flip of her black hair.

"I wish I was comatose," I replied. "You're a terrible storyteller, you know."

She turned to face me and her gaze blazed crimson. "I do not tell *stories*, Madeline. My pain is not for your entertainment."

"I'm tired," I told her. "You're never going to turn me. No matter what you tell me, I will not betray this world, the Druids, or the Lady of the Lake."

Why didn't she just force me to do her bidding?

Morgana had the power to arrive in my memories with a single touch, yet she hadn't even reached beyond the bars of my cage. If she chose, she could draw out my Dark Triune and make it dominant.

She wasn't playing with me—nothing about this was enjoyable for her—so it had to be something else. Morgana wasn't absolute, she had limits.

She couldn't force me.

"How didn't I see it until now?" I murmured with a shake of my head. "*Of course.*"

"Do tell me your thoughts, Madeleine," she purred. "I would like to know what you find so enlightening."

"You can't read my mind, can you?" I laughed. "Not without giving my powers back, and if you do that… You can't turn me if my Natural and Druid Triunes are active. Two good will always outweigh the bad."

She knew I wouldn't break easily. The next time she came to visit my prison, it wouldn't be pleasant. Torture was the next item on the list, and I had to be ready to withstand it.

"This revenge plot of yours is futile," I said, pushing the nausea in my stomach down. "You may destroy the Naturals, but you won't win against the Druids and you will *never* win against the Lady of the Lake."

"We shall see, Triune," the Celestial spat. "I will have what is owed to me, and I will take it no matter the cost."

I rolled my eyes. "Wake up. The universe owes you *shite all.*"

"You claim to be pure, yet you have so much hate in your heart," she scoffed. "You and I aren't that different, Madeleine Greenbriar."

I stood, my knees shaking. Walking over to the bars, I met her gaze and willed her to see the truth in my words. "I don't hate you, Morgana. *I pity you.*" Her eyes narrowed. "And you and I are not the same. We could never be alike."

A smile tugged at her lips as her power crawled along her skin, crimson flame lighting her eyes with the light of the universe. Instead of the glory and benevolence I'd seen within the Lady, all I saw was hatred.

"Where's Elijah?" I demanded.

"He's well cared for, Madeleine."

"*Where is he?*"

"He wasn't hard to break," she told me. "My progeny prepared his soul perfectly."

My hands wrapped around the bars of my cage. "*Bitch.*"

Morgana laughed, the sound of her voice crackling with restrained fire. She approached the cage and leaned towards me, her breath playing across my face.

"You'll see him again," she murmured. "I promise."

I stared, my gaze caught in hers, and felt her magnetic pull on my Dark Triune. *There were truths in her lies.*

"The time for retribution is near," she whispered. "And you will be by my side when I deliver the final blow to this world, and those that come after."

Her eyes were full of starlight and death—and promise of the destruction to come.

My knees buckled and I slid to the ground

Not long after Morgana left, some twisted ex-Camelot demons came to drag the rotting Demon-Flame away.

I was glad for the stink to be gone, but nothing else about my predicament was a cause for celebration. If I believed Morgana, Elijah had been turned, his scarred soul the perfect way to drive Darkness back into him.

I allowed myself a moment to cry, stifling my sobs on my sleeve, then I pulled myself together. The Lady of the Lake had told me I was on the right path, but how could this be the way to end Morgana's plans of destruction?

Everyone back at Camelot was counting on me— my parents, Issac and Greer, Aiden and Amanda, Thompson, Ramona, Trent and Maisy…*everyone*.

In the gloom, I'd lost all sense of time. There was no telling how long I'd been in this cage, but the rumbling in the pit of my stomach had turned into an uncomfortable churning, so I knew it had been at least a few days, maybe a week. My throat was raw and my nose dripped constantly.

I didn't know how long I'd been watched when

movement stirred in the shadows. A familiar form emerged, approaching the bars of my cage, and my heart leapt into my throat.

"*Elijah.*" I pushed to my feet, my entire body aching, as I shuffled towards the bars. "Elijah?"

He stared at me, unmoving. He was wearing his black Natural uniform, his arondight blade at his hip. A glint of silver shone on his right and I held my breath when I realised he had my sword as well.

He'd come to me like this long ago underneath Ben Nevis, but this time his trademark humour was gone. In its place was a coldness that was unfamiliar.

"I know you can still feel our connection, even if I can't." I reached through the bars, but my fingers weren't long enough to touch him. "*I love you.*"

He fisted his hands in his hair. "Shut up, shut up, *shut up.*"

At first I thought he was talking to me, but his eyes weren't focused. He began to pace, his footsteps quickening as his anxiety rose.

"We have to get out of here before Morgana returns," I pleaded. "Please, Elijah. You have to fight the Darkness. She cut me off from my Triune so I can't help you, but I know you're strong. You survived your Colour bomb, remember? If you can get through that, you can get through anything."

Elijah snarled and his arm shot through the bars. His fingers curled around my throat and tightened.

"She is inside me," he raged. "There was nothing I could do. Not even these stupid runes could stop her.

My soul is damaged. My soul is Dark. It's my destiny to betray."

"No, it's not!" I rasped. "Your destiny is to reclaim your birthright from those who took it from you. You are a Druid, Elijah. You are *Colour*."

He let me go with a strangled cry and speared his fingers into his hair. He was pure rage and longing. A war was raging inside him and I wasn't sure who was winning.

"Morgana will destroy everything if we don't do something," I murmured. "If any part of you still loves me, you will help me escape. Together we will end this and save our people. Light *and* Colour."

"I failed," he moaned. "I failed *you*."

"No," I crooned. "You could *never* fail me. This is all her."

He leaned back against the far wall and slid to the floor. He watched me for a long time, his eyes never leaving me.

I wished I could reach out and touch him and tell him everything would be all right. I wished I could use my Triune and force Morgana's influence out of him. I wished I could repair his soul. I wished for a lot of things in those moments.

Exhaustion burned in my legs and I slumped against the bars. What could I say that he already didn't know? If he could break through the Celestial's control, he could free me and it wouldn't be too late to return to Camelot to get Issac's spirit bomb.

Elijah stood, the abrupt movement sending a jolt

through my heart. He reached though the bars and took my hand, jerking me out of the cage like a rag doll. The bars shimmered as I passed through them, the illusion slicing through my body like barbed icicles.

I stumbled and fell against his chest, his closeness jarring. He shoved me back like my touch had burned him, and he narrowed his eyes.

I was having another déjà vu moment and wondered if Elijah realised this was exactly how things had gone the last time we were in the same position. *We had to stop meeting like this.*

"Follow me before I change my mind," he told me in a cool tone.

I wasn't about to argue.

As I followed him out of the alcove, I tripped over the uneven floor, my uncoordinated steps frustrating me no end. Whatever the Dark had done to my cage, it also extended to the caves…but what unsettled me more was the lack of movement. It seemed like the whole place had emptied out.

"Where is everyone?" I whispered.

Elijah didn't reply, he just continued through the tunnel, leading me to who knew where.

Soon we emerged inside a cavern, the ceiling and floor dripping with stalagmites and stalactites. When I hesitated, Elijah dragged me into another opening.

This tunnel was smoother, the rock worn by heavy traffic. No one challenged us. No one crept out of the shadows. No one attacked.

We were alone.

Finally, we emerged from the underground. I

gasped as chilled air hit my skin and sensation rushed at me all at once. The moment my Triune flooded back into my body, warmth spread through my limbs and my hunger pains subsided, as well as the throbbing pain in my joints.

Looking out across the vista before us, I realised we were on a mountainside, but not just any mountain. *Ben Nevis.*

The sun was rising, casting flame across the patchy sky. Any other time, it would have been beautiful, but now all I saw was the long and arduous path before me.

Snow coated the rocky outcrop by the cave entrance, and I fell to my knees. Scooping the white powder into my mouth, I savoured the water as the ice melted on my tongue.

Elijah stared down at me, his gaze as cold as the air around us. Leaving the cave had done nothing to sever Morgana's hold over him.

Rising, I wrapped my fingers around his wrist and poured my power into him. I was forced to jerk my hand back as a wall of Dark spat and crackled. His prism was still there, but it was unresponsive. His Colours were red and angry, but every so often I sensed a spike of blue trying to push past the barrier.

Elijah was still in there but could only reach me enough to set me free. Knowing that gave me hope.

"Hurry," he said. "There is no time left. The Dark marches on Camelot as we speak."

I faltered, my heart jarring. "The city is under attack?"

"Go," he urged, handing me my arondight blade. "I am lost."

I knew we'd had this conversation many times, but I plead with him anyway, *"Come with me."*

"I cannot." His response was bland and unfeeling.

I wound my fingers around my wrist, but the prism he'd given me wouldn't flare. We couldn't end like this… I wouldn't allow it.

"I'll come back for you," I whispered. "I will always find you."

Elijah shook his head. "Don't look back…" he said. "Lest the Dark swallow you whole."

14

This call cannot be connected. Please check the number and try again.

I cried out in frustration and tossed the mobile phone onto the passenger seat of the stolen car I was currently driving one-handed down the motorway. I wove through traffic, flashing the lights and thumping my fist down on the horn to get cars to move out of my way.

It was a wonder I hadn't triggered a police chase, but there were more than a few fists and colourful words flying my way to compensate.

It was in times like these that I wished I was a Flame so I could fly to Camelot.

There is no time left. The Dark marches on Camelot as we speak. Elijah's last words played in my mind, my heart aching over his loss. I'd free him from Morgana's possession, but right now, a legion of demons were approaching the city and I couldn't get ahold of anyone. The only number I remembered was Issac's and it wasn't connecting.

Please don't be too late, I pleaded. *Please…*

It felt like an age before I passed into Shropshire. The sun was high, peeking through a mottled sky. Blue shimmered amongst grey clouds laden with rain and ice—the first glimpse of the heavens since the first snow had fallen. I didn't believe in omens anymore, at least not today.

I was forced to dump the car on a twisty lane near Clee Hill. Leaving it behind with a silent apology to the poor human I nicked it from, I vaulted over a low stone fence and legged it across the springy heath.

My Triune flared as I ran across the field, calling out to the city beyond the veil. The illusion shimmered as I passed through, the hill disappearing, revealing another hidden rise before it. A dozen more steps and I was at the top.

The moment I saw the smoke rising from Camelot, my heart twisted with dread. *She was already here.*

Fire rose from within the lower ruins, crawling up the tiers to the upper echelons of the city. The castle was teeming with Dark essence, and I sensed a malevolence that could only be Morgana within it.

Directly below, Naturals swarmed past the wall, fleeing the flames. Flashes of arondight blades glinted through the haze as they crossed the hillside where I'd raised the lava to protect the city against Ikakantor and his army.

I should have been here to protect them. I'd played right into Morgana's hand and now Camelot was overrun.

I took a step towards the chaos, my anger threatening to break my hold on my Triune. Was this what it was like the day of the cataclysm? I blinked as my vision blurred and I fancied I could see the castle tearing apart as an eruption of Darkness shot into the air from the rift.

How much destruction could Camelot take before it was torn down completely?

"Madeleine!"

I turned at the frenzied shout and my expression fell into one of relief when I saw a familiar form powering up the hill towards me.

"Issac," I cried.

"Madeleine!" He rushed to meet me, his eyes wild. Soot clung to his hair and was smeared across his face. The battle must have been swift and filthy. "We've been searching for you for days."

"I was captured," I said, quickly filling him in.

Issac's eyes widened. "Flames?"

I nodded, but it didn't seem to matter now. If Morgana had led the assault, then they were out of play.

Instead of elaborating, I asked, "Where is everyone?"

"Evacuating," he said, his breath vaporising on the chilled air. "Greer will meet us as soon as she can."

I took a step towards Camelot, my hand reaching for my arondight blade. I was honour bound to fight.

There would be injured Naturals who needed help getting out.

Issac grabbed my wrist and hauled me back. "Madeleine, there's nothing you can do. We have to retreat."

"*I can't leave them.*"

"You have to," he snarled. "I know you think your Triune makes you invincible, but *you can be killed.*"

"It doesn't matter," I snapped. "What good is it if I can't help those who are suffering?" I pointed to the city where a cloud of Dark essence gathered above the castle. "If I leave them behind, they will not survive."

"The city is overrun," he said. "I want to go back too, but what good would it do if we all died right here and now?"

The wind tore at my hair, throwing it in all directions. "We would die knowing we were protecting our brothers and sisters."

Issac pulled me close, his eyes full of fire. "We have a bigger target," he murmured. "*Morgana.* Kill her and we kill the lot of them."

I stared at him, my breath catching.

"We can't stay out in the open," he said. "We have to retreat and wait for Greer's command."

I looked back at Camelot where the cloud was gathering form and momentum. The castle was carved into the side of the cliff, but the Darkness slithered up the rock and over the top, before tipping over the edge at the rear of the crumbled towers. It swirled and heaved like a wild beast hungry for the hunt.

"What is that?" I peered at the mass as my Dark Triune clawed at the Light and Colour overwhelming it.

"Demons without form," Issac said. "Infernals, greater demons, lesser, and kinds we've never seen before."

"Morgana is calling her creatures to fight," I murmured.

"Taking the city was only the first step. Next, she'll come for us." Issac grasped my arm again and tugged me away from the rise. "Now is the time, Madeleine, but we have to wait for the others first."

I allowed him to lead me away from Camelot. My heart ached, not only for Elijah, but for the Naturals who had likely perished in the assault.

He was right. There was nothing we could do.

I threw one last glance over my shoulder and whispered a prayer for the lost. "*May the Light guide you to eternal peace.*"

15

I stood on the hillside overlooking Camelot, watching the swirling cloud of Darkness spiral around the castle. I felt a tear roll down my cheek as I leaned under an outcrop of rock to conceal myself from the demons below.

The sound of boots crunching on hardened snow drew my gaze back. Issac stood beside me, his hands buried deep inside the pockets of his camouflaged coat.

"Elijah didn't return with you?" he asked.

I shook my head. I felt the Druid's absence even more in the silence and the scene below wasn't helping things, either.

"They came out of nowhere," Issac told me. "We had no warning. All our preparations were in vain." He shuffled from foot to foot. "Our hope was foolish."

I disagreed—it wasn't foolish to hope, even when it seemed like there was none.

"She must have gathered every last demon in the

country," I murmured. "Defending against a Celestial was a long shot, but that many Dark creatures…? You were lucky to escape with your lives."

"The other Sanctums were dealing with their own demon problems, but I doubt having them here would have made any difference."

"I'm sorry I wasn't there."

"It wasn't your fault." He took my hand in his, but his gaze never left Camelot. "You were captured."

"We played right into her hands. They were waiting for us to leave the city," I told him. "She was never on Earth, Issac. She made her own Flames."

He looked at me, his expression troubled. "Where *is* Elijah?"

"It's like you said," I whispered. "His soul… It was too easy. He let me out too easily." If the Dark had a hold of him as completely as I feared, then… "Morgana said I'd see him again, then he showed up and freed me."

"Perhaps you're right," Issac said with a frown. "Either she underestimated his feelings for you or it's a trap. She knows you will come with the flower and if she can take it, we'll have nothing."

"Regardless, I have to rescue him," I said. "He would do the same for me."

"Luckily, I can help you in that department." Issac reached into his pocket and took out a familiar slice of crystal. *The flower.*

I gasped and reached out for the shard. "You still have it?"

"Ramona named it the Spirit Bloom," he told me. "But this is only one piece of it."

"Only a piece?" I frowned, turning over the quartz. It was smaller than I remembered and a milky smear imbedded deep within was where I expected the flower to be. "I don't understand. Where's the rest of it?"

"We kept working after you were captured," he murmured. "The flower has four petals, each holding enough potency to do the job four times over."

My eyes widened. "You made four spirit bombs."

Issac nodded, smiling for the first time since I arrived. "I have one, Ramona another, and Greer has the third."

"Is this the fourth?"

"Yes, and it's yours." He pressed the crystal shard into my palm and curled my fingers around it.

"How does it work?"

"You'll need to stab it into her heart and use your spirit to ignite the bloom," he explained.

"So, it's an up-close-and-personal experience." I slipped the crystal into my pocket and made sure the zipper was closed. "I assume I have to peel my spirit away from my body to blow her up."

"Yes, exactly like you did when you exorcised those Infernals."

I had so many questions, but the sound of Ramona's voice silenced me.

"Madeleine?"

I strode across the snow and threw my arms

around her neck. The doctor returned the gesture, stroking her hand over my hair.

"Are you all right?" she asked. "I'm glad you're here."

"I don't know," I replied truthfully, "but we're alive for now."

We embraced a moment longer before she drew back. "Greer has arrived," she murmured. "She'd like to see you."

I swallowed hard. "Then we better go. We have a lot to do."

Greer was waiting for us on the other side of the rise, concealed by a ward so thick even I had trouble seeing through it.

Aiden was with her, his expression greyish as he wrung his hands together.

"Madeleine, I'm so glad to see you." She looked over my shoulder. "Elijah?"

"I had to leave him behind," I whispered.

Her expression fell, but she remained calm, even in the face of so much destruction. "You escaped Morgana's grasp, so there is still hope. Tell us…what happened?"

I wasted no time telling them what Morgana had revealed, leaving nothing out, not even my last meeting with Elijah outside the caves at Ben Nevis. When I was finished, there was a long stretch of silence. The only sound that broke through the dread was the demonic wailing of the Darkness enveloping the city below.

Greer opened her mouth to speak, but whatever

she was about to say was interrupted by the sudden appearance of Caleb Thompson.

He knelt before Greer, his chest heaving. "Our forces have scattered amongst the hills," he said. "They're concealed and awaiting orders."

She looked to me, her expression grave. If anyone understood what we faced right now, it was Greer. We were at a precipice.

"We have one chance," she murmured. "We have to—" Her words were cut off, and she clutched her chest. With a cry, she fell to her knees, her face contorted in pain.

"Greer?" I knelt before her and lay my hands on her face. The moment my skin touched hers, a flash of Light seared my mind and I jerked away.

"*She…*" the Inquisitor rasped. "*I can feel them all…*"

"The Codex," Aiden declared. "Morgana has the Codex!"

"How in the bloody hell did she get it?" Thompson raged. "It was hidden for this very reason!"

The Codex wasn't just a book. It held the entire known history of the Naturals and was so infused with Light, it connected every single soul that contained Light of its own. The protector was entwined with it like no other artefact, and through it, Greer was a conduit—only she could touch it without bursting into flames. The Codex guided and advised through the power it held from centuries of tales, but it could also give Morgana everything she needed to kill every last one of us.

All she had to do was destroy it and we'd all drop dead.

"It's how she's going to destroy us," I murmured, the gravity of what was happening hitting home. "The Codex is connected to all of us through Greer." My fingers hovered in the air beside her cheek.

"If she destroys the book, she will destroy us all," Aiden said, shaking his head.

"It's now or never," Greer managed to rasp. "Morgana has to die today or we have lost everything." Her gaze fixed on mine. "*Madeleine…* you know what to do."

I rose and began to pace, my anxiety threatening to send my Triune into instability. The Dark was fighting inside me, begging to be unleashed.

Issac stood before me, cutting off my path. "Madeleine."

"*Stop*," I hissed. "My Triune…"

Issac peered at me, understanding that I was struggling. "Give us a moment," he said to the others. "We're asking a lot from her."

"I understand, but we have no time," Aiden noted. "If we could shoulder this burden together, we would."

"I know what I have to do," I said, my voice trembling. "But give me a moment. It's a lot. I need a second to scream at the universe before I face off with death."

The Naturals lowered their gazes and Greer smiled, the heel of her palm still pressing over her heart. She understood I needed a moment to gather myself before the battle to come. She would give me this, even though she would feel the deaths of a thousand Naturals before she died.

I wished I could have thanked her in that moment, but it seemed there was a lot of wishing going around. Now I had to figure out what to do.

Issac guided me away from the group and we stood on the rise together. Below, smoke billowed from within Camelot's walls. Morgana was hard at work, redecorating the city to suit her apocalyptic taste.

"What if I can't contain the explosion?" I whispered. "What if I fail?"

"I trust you, Madeleine," Issac said. "But it's more than that… *I believe in you*. I believe you can do this. Like Arondight and Excalibur before you, I believe this is your destiny."

Destiny. What in the world did I know about destiny?

"Morgana said I could choose. That because I was a Triune, I had three paths. What if I pick the wrong one?"

Issac smiled and lay a hand on my shoulder. "You really believe what Morgana has to say?"

He had a good point. How much of her story was painted with truth, and how much of it was lies? It could be all or none, or maybe a little of each. Something broke inside her when she took on flesh and bone, but it didn't give her the right to tear apart the universe in her lust for ultimate revenge.

"Elijah knows about our plan," I said instead. "Morgana will know I'm coming with the flower."

"That's why I'm going with you."

"Issac, no," I declared. "You—"

"Won't be expected," he interrupted. "Elijah knows you, Madeleine. He'll assume you won't let anyone die and come alone."

"But she'll know you're with me the moment we enter Camelot. Morgana's power is absolute, Issac. We can't hope to fool her."

"We can," he said with a smile.

My brow furrowed. "How?"

"With your parents' crystals." He reached into his pocket and retrieved a quartz crystal cluster.

I stared at the clear stone, my heart pounding. "My parents?"

"They figured it out, Madeleine. They know how Camelot's illusions work."

Dad was excited about creating crystal batteries with the help of the barriers left behind by the Naturals of Camelot, but I never thought they'd work it out this quickly. I blinked and pressed my hand over the quartz. The Lady of the Lake told me I was on the right path, but here I was thinking it was all about me. I would deliver the final blow, but we all had a part to play in our final stand.

"Where are they?" I murmured.

"They're safe," Issac replied. "They're on their way to Glastonbury with all other nonessential personnel. They'll be protected there."

I sighed, my heartbeat slowing. Glastonbury was the site of the ancient catacombs and had once been a sacred place for the Druids before they left Earth. It was also used as a prison, but that meant it was heavily fortified and secret. A small comfort, at least.

Issac closed his hand over mine, encasing the crystal. "She'll sense you, but I'll be masked."

I understood his plan. Morgana would likely take my spirit bomb away from me and Issac would be there to give his. It was a sorely needed failsafe.

The only way to win against a creature as absolute as Morgana, was to trick her.

"If this is your plan, then why tell me?" I asked, slipping my had away from the crystal. "She will know all of it the moment she touches me."

"Because I will be by your side the entire time. We will hit hard and fast. Ideally, you'll be the one to strike the blow and contain the explosion. I'm only there in case things go sideways."

I looked up at him, my eyes misting with tears. In the valley beyond, the demonic essence wailed, a constant reminder of what we faced. We were about to walk into a storm like no one had ever seen before.

"Everyone has to leave," I murmured. "If the blast breaks free…" I took a deep breath and pressed my trembling palms against my thighs. "There's a chance none of us will come back, Issac. It's all or nothing. Death or triumph."

"I know," he told me. "If we fail, we die knowing we did everything in our power to save the world. That's what sacrifice is. Someone has to stand up and risk losing it all for the safety of others. May as well be us, right?"

I heaved in a shaking breath and a tear fell from my eye. It was hard to believe that I was standing here after all I'd been through. To be demoted to guard duty at Camelot for being disobedient, distrusted and shunned for almost turning into a demon-hybrid, to becoming a Triune with the fate of the world in my hands.

"Don't fret," Issac said. "If we ball this up, there are two more spirit bombs waiting in the wings."

I nodded but didn't tell him my other fear. If we failed, we may not get another chance. Morgana would destroy the Codex, Wilder and Scarlett would never wake, and the Naturals would cease to be.

Greer was right. We had no time. We had to strike…or die trying.

And who would walk out of this at the end was all up to me.

There was no time for goodbyes.

Greer held my hand and murmured a prayer while Aiden cradled her trembling body. They huddled together amongst the rocks while Thompson headed out to relay her command to the Naturals scattered amongst the hills.

The Dark would be coming, and they had to be ready.

"We just need enough time to get into the castle," Issac said. "It will all be over soon."

"One way or another," Greer whispered.

"If we can't kill Morgana, we'll get the Codex," I told her. "No matter what."

Issac knelt beside Greer and Aiden. "You have to evacuate to Glastonbury," he told them. "If the blast breaks past Madeleine's barrier, you'll both be lost." His gaze flicked to Greer. "Do you understand?"

She nodded and took his hand. "Issac—"

"It's okay," he interrupted. "I know what I'm doing."

I thought of the last words Merlin spoke to me through the portal to the Darklands. *Slán, Trí Anam. Ádh mór. Farewell, Triune. Good luck…*

"*Ádh mór,*" I whispered.

"We'll see you soon," Aiden said to us. "We'll wait for you in Glastonbury."

Issac nodded and turned to me. "Well, then," he said, "we better not linger. Destiny awaits."

16

Issac and I lingered outside Camelot's outer wall, staring into what used to be the base camp. Every scrap of Natural habitation was gone, and in its place was a twisted jumble of rock split into three paths.

"It's gone," I said, stating the obvious. "All of it."

Issac looked towards the darkening sky. "Can you feel that?"

My Triune vibrated and I nodded. "They're out there. Waiting…" *For me to knock on the door, most likely.*

"The demons will be stronger," he said. "They have their power back."

I brushed my hand over the twisted stone, my palm rasping over scratchy yellow lichen. It reminded me of the way Scarlett had described Camelot when she and Wilder had first arrived here, back when the rift was still open. Darkness had contorted the city into a nightmarish maze patrolled by powerful demons.

I'd fought them on several occasions, but the ex-residents of Camelot were much removed from what they once were. Without a link to the One—the Dark creature that made them—they'd spent the last six years wasting away.

"This doesn't look familiar," I murmured, looking down one fork of the path.

"It's a labyrinth," Issac said. "The illusions have been twisted by the influx of Darkness."

"A maze made out of Camelot… Easy. We both know the city. It's changed, but it's still the same at its core."

"It's not that simple," he said with a shake of his head. "Mazes have more than one route, labyrinths only have one."

"Things are never easy in this world." I sighed and began to look for clues.

I tried to sense which path called to me more, but they all felt the same, so I poked about in the grass, scratching at the moss with a stick.

"Very creative," Issac said, "but I think we're just going to have to pick a path and rely in faith for this one."

I tossed the stick and heaved out another sigh. "Typical."

Issac was about to choose a path when a mark on a stone caught my eye. I picked at the lichen and my heart leapt. It was a rune! A long vertical line with four horizontal lines emerging from its right side. *Saille*. Willow.

I tugged on his sleeve. "Issac, *look*."

"Willow," he said, his eyes widening. "It's one of Galahad's runes."

The knight of Camelot, Lancelot's son, who helped Scarlett find her way through the past to Avalon…and risked his life to mark the way through the Dark's labyrinth. I wondered if Elijah had met him. I bit my bottom lip at the thought of the Druid.

"They're still here," I whispered, shaking off my despair. "Maybe we have a way to the castle after all."

Issac patted his pocket, checking that his crystal was still firmly in place, and wasted no time venturing into the labyrinth. Treading carefully, we followed the path marked by the willow rune. Scarlett trusted Galahad then, and we had the same faith now.

We would find our way, but the rest was up to us.

I cast my hearing out, listening for anything Dark patrolling the twisted city. If Aiden saw this, he'd have a meltdown. The lower city was completely unrecognisable…if we were still in the lower city, that was.

The deeper we moved, the longer the shadows grew. The stone sparkled like it was covered in a fine layer of crushed crystal, the absence of colour reminding me of the Darklands. This place and that black landscape weren't the same, but the similarities were startling. Perhaps we were all descended from the Old Ones in a round-about way, but something told me it wasn't for the likes of us to know the answers to those questions.

I sensed movement ahead just as I spotted another willow rune. I pushed a startled Issac back into an alcove and threw up a hasty barrier to cover our location as the sound of claws scratching against stone began to approach.

We held our breath as the menacing footsteps grew louder. *Clack, scrape. Clack, scrape.*

Then, it came into view.

Everyone had heard the stories about the creatures that dwelt in the rift-infested Camelot, but seeing them in person was shocking. These monsters were the same that emerged from the way between worlds and slaughtered every Natural in their path… then had ventured out into the world to hunt them—and the Druids—down one by one.

The demon slithered down the passage, its black hide shimmering in the strange light. Gangly arms and legs carried its elongated body as it lumbered down the path, it's almost non-existent lips pulled back to reveal the rows upon rows of sharpened teeth set into its jaw.

With direct access to Morgana's power, it had grown an extra three feet and its slender arms and chest bulked into sinewy muscle. No wonder the Naturals had been forced to retreat when the Celestial arrived with her followers in tow. A swarming army of these things would have decimated them in seconds.

I looked at Issac and I saw a flicker of fear in his eyes that startled me. He was one of the strongest Naturals I knew, his calm demeanour was meant to ground me.

He cupped my cheek and I felt his Light warm the edges of my mind. I opened up to him and his voice echoed, "They came over the hill. One thousand screaming monsters just like that one. Morgana was at their centre, her twisted starlight feeding their Darkness."

"Courage," I told him. "The castle isn't far."

We waited until the demon turned a corner, then we ducked out of the alcove, following the way the rune pointed.

No one challenged us, even though Darkness clung to every surface. Eyes watched our progress, keeping to the shadows. They were out there, salivating and longing to spill blood, but none approached. It seemed like we'd been granted safe passage.

Soon the castle loomed out of the mist ahead, the courtyard smashed and melted from the force of Morgana's starlight.

We looked up at the interior of the castle, knowing the Celestial was waiting at the top. The floors had been exposed centuries ago when the rift had torn the structure apart. This was the closest I'd ever been, and now we were about to go inside the ancestral home of the Pendragon Naturals—Wilder's family.

Issac found a spiral staircase inside the lower floor, and we climbed together, our boots slipping on the worn steps.

Honestly, the anticipation over the fight was making my stomach churn…and not in a good way.

We finally made it to the top where the uppermost floor was completely open to the sky.

Morgana lounged on a throne of melted stone, her skin glowing with muted crimson starlight as she gazed over her ruined kingdom. She was waiting for us.

Her lip curled in triumph as Issac and I stood before her. The Celestial had crowned herself Queen of Camelot and was taking perverse delight in granting us an audience.

"Your Highn-*arse*," I drawled. "I see you've made yourself right at home."

"So confident," the Celestial said. "I see you still hold the same misguided attitude you had while in my dungeon. Though I'm pleased to see Elijah knows his place. He can follow orders after all."

I narrowed my eyes and didn't reply. So, I was right to be wary about my 'escape'. I loved Elijah, but while he was under Morgana's control, I couldn't trust him, not completely.

"Do you really believe it was your cunning that brought you here unscathed? *Both* of you." She laughed and rose from her throne. "Your little crystal fooled my demons, but it would never fool me. I wanted you to come. I wanted you to see what happens when you defy me, Madeleine."

"Throwing a temper tantrum when you can't get your way isn't impressive," I drawled. "It's pathetic."

Her gaze moved to Issac and lingered. Clearly, she liked what she saw.

"I have a special pet, too," she purred. Raising her hand, she grinned as Elijah stepped out of the shadows and stood at her side.

My heart leapt and I took a step forwards, but Issac grasped my wrist.

"Don't," he said. "He's Dark. I can feel it."

Morgana's smile widened. "Your Natural will look good on my other arm." Her teeth tugged at her bottom lip. "A Druid on the right and a Natural on the left...and a Dark creature at my feet." She laughed at her own cunning. "I will have a Triune of my own."

I wrapped my hand around my wrist and called on the prism, begging for Elijah to hear me. Our souls were connected through our love and no one could come between us, not even Morgana. I had to believe it. He'd come back to me through Ikakantor's possession and had fought across worlds to be with me. I'd fight to the end if it meant he'd live.

I sent a silent plea to the prism linking us. *He had to hear me.*

"Where's the Codex?" I demanded, trying to keep Morgana talking. I had to find a way to get close and stab the bitch in the heart, but Elijah and Issac had to get some distance first.

Morgana waved her hand, revealing a concealed pedestal beside her throne. The illusion wavered and she rolled her eyes. "What a pathetic little thing it is."

"You will give it back, even if I have to pry it from your dead hands," I snarled.

"How stupid are you people?" she declared. "You infused a book with so much essence it connected you as one. You made yourselves vulnerable to death with one strike." She cackled, the sound bouncing off the stone walls. "You made it so easy, it's laughable!"

I tightened my grip on my wrist and glanced at Elijah. A slight touch of Colour sparked underneath my skin and he nodded, the movement undetected by Morgana. She was too busy basking in her rant to take any notice. *Shite, she was an arrogant woman.*

"I disagree," Issac said. "Together we are stronger. Isn't that right, Madeleine?"

I glanced at him before returning my gaze to Elijah's. "There's a saying in our world that I think is appropriate in this moment. *Love conquers all.*"

The Druid moved fast, striking Morgana on the back of her neck with a heavy blow that took her by surprise. She roared with rage and hurled a blast of energy at him.

A split-second distraction was all I needed. As Elijah hurtled across the room, I ran for the Codex.

"I'll kill you all!" Morgana shrieked as Issac attempted to draw her ire.

I kicked the pedestal, sending the Codex flying across the room. It skidded over broken tiles, the cover snagging and tearing, and Morgana let out an unearthly wail that grated against my Triune.

"I don't need you," she shouted, her starlight igniting. "I can get into Avalon other ways."

"Not if I have anything to do with it." I engaged my arondight blade and pushed away the uncomfortable feeling. "Your reign of terror ends today, Morgana."

I attacked, pouring my Triune into my blade. The

sword sparked with Light and Colour as I pushed the Darkness away, and I brought it around in a savage arc aimed at Morgana's neck.

The Celestial's hand shot up and grasped the blade, essence erupting around us as our power clashed. She wrenched the hilt out of my grasp and lashed out with her other arm.

I let the crystal slip into my palm and I ducked underneath her blow, then thrust the spirit bomb towards her heart.

I almost had her when Morgana's knee slammed into my stomach. I gasped, taken off guard by the unexpected blow. Winded, I collapsed to my knees and the crystal fell to the floor, a delicate tinkling sound echoed around the stone chamber.

"Do you think this little thing could stop me?" Morgana's boot stomped the crystal, the quartz shattering with a crack, and I reached towards it with a cry of anguish. "Your struggle is for *nothing*. Your kind will be forgotten, Madeleine Greenbriar. *I will make sure of it*."

"You're not a saviour," I rasped. "You're a *monster*."

Her lip curled into a snarl. "You would try to erase me? I would gladly return the favour."

The Celestial wrapped her hands around my neck and squeezed. She bore down on me, her starlight burning through my mind, eroding everything it touched. I was nothing against her might.

Morgana was absolute.

All the impossible deeds I'd done were forgettable.

The terrible power of the universe bloomed behind her eyes, consuming and remaking me anew.

This was it. Death was upon us all. *I'd failed…*

As my vision began to falter, Issac pushed between us, breaking Morgana's hold on me. His sword flared as she grasped the blade in her hand, crimson flames sparking from her flesh.

I scrambled backwards and reached for my hilt as Issac dropped his blade. That's when I saw the flash of crystal in his hand.

Behind me, I felt Elijah move towards the Codex, but I didn't turn, my gaze frozen on the spirit bomb. Dread pulled at my Dark Triune, but it was too late.

As Issac slammed the crystal shard into Morgana's chest, I screamed.

What came next happened so fast I wasn't sure it was entirely real. Issac's gaze met mine and the castle blurred around us. *He'd ignited the spirit bomb.*

Lunging, I threw up my arms and unleashed my Triune. A tremendous amount of power flowed through me, filling my veins with a raging fire I'd never felt before. A barrier flared into life, swirling with Colour, Light…and Darkness. For the first time, all three shards of my soul had entwined and manifested together.

I was blinded, my physical body a conduit for something far outside my realm of understanding. Finally, I realised that Morgana had been telling the truth about me. I could ascend to live as essence amongst the stars if I chose, but there my power would be a terrible burden. My body was the only thing keeping it in check.

Stars burst through my vision and I gasped as the flow of power ceased. It felt as if someone had pressed pause on the whole scene. The castle faded, the world enshrouding with white mist.

Disoriented, I lowered my arms, wondering if we'd failed and if this was what death looked like. I blinked and realised that it wasn't the afterlife. This was the in-between place between life and erasure.

Footsteps echoed behind me and I turned to find Issac emerge from the mist.

I choked back a sob. "Issac, *no…*"

He smiled and cupped my cheek. "I had to," he murmured. "Please don't be angry."

His skin was chilling as his soul slipped away and I began to sob.

"We were supposed to walk out of here together," I choked out. "You were supposed to go to New York and lead the Sanctum. You were——"

"*Shh,*" he crooned. "It's okay, Madeleine. This was my destiny."

"It's a pretty sucky destiny."

He chuckled softly, then pulled me close. When his lips met mine, my heartbeat sped up. His kiss was soft and full of love…and a final goodbye.

"I just wanted to do that once before the end," he whispered as he faded. "*Just once.*"

Time sped up as I was forced back into my body. The barrier wavered as the bomb completed its ignition and detonated.

Morgana's lips parted as her body began to tear apart, and the scream she let out shook the entire city. Crimson starlight bloomed within as her soul burned, then she shattered.

The explosion was terrifying, the force of the blast almost buffeting me off my feet. Stone crumbled and fell around us, the castle disintegrating as I held the barrier.

I pushed against it with all my strength, a scream tearing from my lips as the blast burned my exposed flesh. The barrier flickered as stone blocks slammed into it and shards hit my shoulders.

White flame billowed before me, burning so bright I was blinded. Then, just as suddenly as it began, the explosion sucked back in on itself…

And everything went dark.

When I opened my eyes, all I saw was ruined stone and a grey sky beyond. The castle still stood, but barely.

It was raining, the misty droplets mixing with the tears staining my cheeks. The scent of scorched earth filled my nostrils and I gasped.

"*Madeleine…*" Elijah cradled my exhausted body, his hands smoothing my hair as his tears fell unchecked.

I opened my mouth, but my voice was frozen. *Is it over?*

"It worked," he murmured. "Morgana's gone, along with her demons."

His gaze was full of anguish and I knew it was true. Issac was gone.

Erased.

"I have the Codex," he whispered. "The Naturals are safe."

I didn't care. I sobbed, my chest heaving as I gasped for air.

All Elijah could do was hold me as the rain fell over us, the ruins of Camelot the only witness to my despair.

17

———

We never made it to Glastonbury.

The moment Morgana's soul was ripped from her body, the Dark fell and the illusions that twisted Camelot disappeared.

Under the command of Caleb Thompson, Naturals emerged from the hills and began to swarm into the city, sweeping every last corner of the ruins to make sure no Darkness lingered.

The sun had long set by the time Elijah and I made it out of the castle.

Light shone from beyond the city, illuminating our path back to what remain of the base camp.

Greer stood at the bottom of the thoroughfare, waiting for us. Naturals lingered in the background, their silent vigil haunting in the aftermath of what had happened at the castle.

Elijah carried the Codex in his bare hands and to her astonishment, handed it back to the only other person, besides the Twin Flames, who could hold the mystical tome without bursting into flame.

"Thank you," she said, clutching the book against her chest. Then she turned to me, her eyes misting with tears. "Issac?"

I shook my head, unable to say the words.

"He was the one…" Elijah told her. "He sacrificed himself to slay Morgana."

The sounds of shocked gasps and distressed murmurings faded into the background as grief threatened to pull me under. It was a moment of celebration, but without Issac, the mood was subdued.

"His soul may be gone, but he will never be forgotten," Greer said, her voice trembling. "What he has done today—"

I didn't hear the rest of her speech. How had he ignited the spirit bomb in the first place? I was the only one who could, so why? *Why, Issac?*

Then a spark of Light ebbed through my despair and I understood.

Issac had studied his whole life to understand souls and spirit. He'd guided me, trained me, and had taught me to enter another person's mind. It was his life's calling to understand his soul. It meant he was the only other person with the skills to ignite the bomb. That was the real reason why he came with me. *To defeat Morgana, we had to trick her.*

It didn't matter if she knew we had more than one spirit bomb. She believed I was the only one who could deliver it and that was her downfall.

The Lady of the Lake had said I'd know what to do with the flower when the time came, but I didn't realise it meant giving it to Issac so he could deliver the final blow.

I glanced at Greer and saw guilt in her eyes. Back on the hill, before we'd gone down to the city, Issac had told her he knew what he was doing. *She knew.* She allowed him to go to his death.

"You knew what he was going to do," I snarled. "You knew he was going to sacrifice himself."

"Madeleine, if there was any other way—"

Trent interrupted her empty excuses as he pushed through the crowd, followed by Maisy, their arondight blades in their hands. I should have been glad to see them, but my heart was numb.

"Aiden asked me to come immediately," Trent said, glancing between us. "We've received word from Glastonbury." From the look on his face, I could tell it wasn't good news.

"The Flames?" Greer asked hopefully.

Trent shook his head. "No change. They are still asleep."

I hissed and turned my ire onto Greer. "*How dare you.* You let him go to this death and now it was all for nothing."

Her eyes widened and I knew my own were a mess of black veins as my Dark Triune threatened to lash out.

"Madeleine, please…" she began.

I roared in anger and strode away from her and the crowd, forging a path back into the city.

"Madeleine, wait!" Elijah followed, the prism on my arm flaring.

"He sacrificed his soul to save us and the Flames are still in a coma!" I shouted. I cried out in anguish and the ground cracked underneath my feet. "Issac erased himself for nothing!" Steam rose from the fissures, melting the snow into slush.

"No, it wasn't for nothing. Issac saved us all."

"Maybe it's me," I said, not hearing him. "Maybe they aren't awake because I'm here." I fumbled at my belt and pulled out my cold iron dagger.

"Madeleine," Elijah hissed, knocking the blade out of my hand. It clattered to the ground, the sound grating against my mind. "It's not you."

"How can you be so sure?" I bent to pick up the dagger, but he grabbed my arm and pulled me to him.

"Because you've always been a Triune," he told me. "It doesn't matter if you never knew, or your Darkness wasn't activated, or any other excuse you're about to spit at me. Souls do not lie. *Ever.*"

I stared at him, not sure which way I was going to fall. I had three directions to choose from—Light, Colour, or Darkness. Elijah sighed and pulled me into his arms.

I pressed my ear to his chest and listened to his heartbeat, my gaze finding the edges of the runes he'd carved into his flesh.

"The Dark always existed alongside the Twin Flames," he murmured, stroking my hair. "It can only mean one thing."

"Morgana's soul isn't gone."

"Yes, a piece of it remains."

I began to shake, the toll of the barrier beginning to manifest through the shock my physical body was experiencing. If Ramona was here, she'd tell me to rest, but it wasn't time for that, not yet.

"Issac did not die for nothing," Elijah whispered. "He understood his destiny at the end. He trained a lifetime for that one moment, whether he knew it or not."

"It's cruel," I said. "He had so much more to give."

"He loved you, Madeleine. He wouldn't want you to mourn him, not like this." I also knew he wouldn't want me to stop fighting.

"Wise words," I murmured, wiping at my tears. "Also unexpected."

"When he was helping me with my Colours after my…incident, we spoke about a lot of things." He worried his bottom lip before he added, "We reached an understanding."

"Did you know?" I asked.

"No, but I think he knew from the beginning." Elijah shook his head. "Now we just have to find the last shred of Morgana's soul and deliver the final blow."

"Just?" I snorted.

"It sounds simple," he said with a shrug, "but it could be anywhere. There are places in this world that are still hidden, even from people like us."

"That narrows it down." I looked up at the castle

and tensed as a vision of Issac appeared in my mind's eye. His goodbye kiss lingered on my lips and I brushed my fingers over them.

I found myself thinking about what he'd do if he were here. Only moments ago, he was beside me and now, he was gone forever.

"I can ask her," I murmured. "If a part of Morgana's soul still clings to life, then I can walk into death and drag it out of her."

Elijah glanced uneasily at the dagger. "Into death?"

"Not like that…not physically. I'm talking about my spirit."

"That doesn't make me feel any better." He stroked my cheek. "The body cannot live without the mind."

"I know, but this might be the only way we can find any answers," I said. "I can go where the subconscious meets the soul, but how is she lingering?" *The Celestial was hanging around like a stain on the carpet that was impossible to get out.*

"So she pulled her spirit away from her body at the last second," Elijah murmured. "Or she had a failsafe…"

"That blast had to have left a mark, but I think it's deeper than that," I said. "She knew what we were up to."

"You don't think…" His eyes widened as he realised the enormity of what could be happening. "Like Ikakantor did with me. Possession?"

My hands shook as dread filled my heart for what

felt like the millionth time that day. The Celestial could be living inside any of us, but that wasn't even the worst thing she could do. Morgana created the Dark—what if she'd done it again, but this time masked it as her resurrection?

"I'm going to wring the truth out of her one way or another," I snarled. "I will gladly walk into death to do it."

"Madeleine." Elijah took my hands in his. "Don't let vengeance cloud your mind. *Please.*"

"I won't." I squeezed his fingers and his prism began to glow. "I understand what my Druid Triune is now. Philomena's gift wasn't fire, it was spirit. The wisdom of the Druids will stay my hand and the Light of the Naturals will guide me home."

Our link deepened and he nodded. "I've heard of Spirit Walkers, but I've never met one," he mused. "It wasn't an ability that was spoken of often. It was seen as sacred. A blessing…and a curse."

I shivered, not liking the sound of that.

"I remember Philomena and her sister, Gilhana, were always considered gifted amongst the Druids," he went on, lost in memory. "Both were priestesses, like the ones you saw at Brionglóid."

"The ritual at the henge? Those were priestesses?"

He nodded. "They study their whole lives to master their Colours."

"It's a romantic notion, but we don't have time for that. I have to go now, or not at all."

"Are you sure?" he murmured. "It's so soon."

I looked up at him. "I have to go back to the

castle…to where Issac died. It has to be now, before the residue from the sprit bomb fades."

He glanced nervously at the light shining from the base camp. "What about Greer? She's still the Inquisitor."

"Screw orders," I snarled. "I know Greer had to keep it from me, but I'm not ready to let it go. He just died, Elijah. It's barely been an hour, and I have to go up there and face the creature who took him from us."

"Okay," he said. "I'll come with you. The Dark may be gone, but I'd feel better if I was there when you walk into death."

The Dark was gone.

I had to stop a moment and realise what we'd done today. Issac was gone, but Morgana's hold over the living was severed and demons everywhere were dead. After over eight hundred years, Darkness was finally eradicated from the Earth.

But it wasn't just our world—it was all of them.

Oh, Issac… You should have been here to see this. I swallowed the lump in my throat and took Elijah's hand.

"Are you okay?" he asked, his brow furrowing.

I nodded and squeezed his hand. "It's time to finish this. Let's go wake up the Twin Flames."

⸻

The castle was shrouded in darkness—actual darkness, this time—as Elijah and I ventured into its ruined depths.

After the force of the explosion, the entire area felt unstable. An uneasiness lay thick in the air as if the whole structure was teetering on the edge of an abyss. Half of the inner keep was carved out of the cliff face, but the other was a jagged spear on one side of the ancient rift. Trust Morgana to pick the precarious side as her throne room.

We climbed the stairs, each step jarring my battered heart. A part of me hoped I'd see Issac one last time, but I knew his soul was already gone. He'd faded away after he'd kissed me in that strange in-between place.

I crossed the room, the wind fluttering against my skin. A few flakes of snow spiralled through the night and melted as they touched my shoulders and hair.

Stopping beside the melted stone throne, I stared at the black marks on the floor. I fancied I could feel something lingering in them, but it was difficult to tell the difference between fantasy and reality, especially in this place.

"Madeleine?"

"This is the place. It has to be." I looked up at Elijah. "She will pay. *I swear it.*"

"Do what you like once you're in there, but I'm tying a rope around you," he stated.

"A rope?"

"If you get caught, I can pull you back."

"Sounds reasonable." I gestured to him. "On with it, then."

He blinked and shook his head. "I already did it."

"You did? When?"

"Were you expecting some kind of fanfare? I can get you some streamers and confetti if you like."

"*Elijah.*"

He shrugged and turned me away from the scorch marks on the floor. "Just trying to lighten the mood. It's been an awful day."

"I'm sorry." I popped up on my tiptoes and kissed him on the cheek. "I'm glad you're here with me."

He smiled, his Colours shimmering. "I'll be here watching over you."

"*Thank you.*"

Pushing aside my anger and fear, I closed my eyes. I focused on the residue from the blast, zeroing in on the part of me that peeled away from my body. My soul stirred, then a cool breeze fluttered against my skin.

I took a step forwards and a shiver passed through my body…and I opened my eyes to another world.

Ivory mist curled around my ankles but beyond it, reality was formless and without colour—otherwise known as completely white. There was no sky, no earth, no plants or life. How I was standing was beyond me. Perhaps it was just my earthly perception that gave my spirit form…and gravity to adhere to.

"I was wondering when I'd see you."

I turned to find Morgana lingering in the mist, her naked body translucent. She appeared to my eyes in the form she took when she emerged from the vault. Her Celestial body sparkled with crimson fire, but it generated no heat.

I guess this was the next closest thing to what she used to be before she took on flesh and bone.

"So, you've worked it out," she continued, prowling towards me. "My soul will cling to the Beyond so long as a piece of me remains in reality."

"It's so nice to see through you," I drawled.

"My heart, my love…" she sighed, "someone to share the dark and lonely days of eternity with." She laughed and shook her head. "It's a little vicarious, but when your soul has been blasted into little more than vapour, one has to improvise."

My heart, my love… She couldn't mean…

"The One," I breathed. "You made another? But how can he still exist when you're dead?"

Morgana smirked triumphantly. "How do your modern humans say it? New and *improved?* Given my recent experiences, I thought it best to make sure there were no gaps in my plan."

"It doesn't matter," I snarled. "I will always be there to stop you."

"I'd like to see you try. In fact, I will be there in *spirit.*" Morgana smirked, looking extremely pleased with herself. "Once he's devoured your world, he will use you and your Triune to break into Thríbhís Mhór and destroy Merlin and his pathetic little creatures. Then all that stands in the way of my eternal peace is Avalon. Once your precious Lady of the Lake is dead, my revenge will be complete."

There was a third Celestial, but I wasn't about to reveal her existence to Morgana. It was entirely possible that one of her earlier plans had failed to eradicate all the Celestials. If so, I had the feeling the unknown woman was to be protected—the Lady of the Lake had hinted as much.

"Where is he?" I demanded. "Where is the One?"

"He will rise when the time comes," she purred, placing her palm on her chest. "My precious heart."

I stepped back as the truth of her words slapped me the face. *Her heart.* Morgana had put her heart into the One. It was her link to reality and the reason why she hadn't truly died.

What would happen if I killed it? Would the Dark be destroyed for good? I began to wonder if that's why the Lady of the Lake lingered in Avalon. If she passed, then the Naturals would die with her.

"Why?" I whispered. "You could just kill the Lady and be done with us all…"

"Enjoyment," Morgana replied with a grin. "I knew there was a reason I liked speaking with you, Madeleine. You understand where others do not. I so despise repeating myself."

I strode towards her with a snarl and wrapped my hand around her throat. Her skin was cool to the touch, her death quenching the celestial blaze within her.

"Where is he?" I demanded. "Where is the One?"

"You will go to him, Madeleine," Morgana purred. "You're the only one who can."

"What?" I whispered.

"And when you do, he will awaken. It's poetic, don't you think? You have an equal chance between destroying everything you love and saving it." Her expression turned thoughtful, then she added, "I think I might just send you to him now. We both know what choice you will make. You're so boring, you know."

My breath caught as I fell, nothingness dragging me through the mist. My fingers scraped the ground, but it was merely the manifestation of my physical mind I was trying to grab. I wasn't really there.

Morgana's laughter followed me through limbo, taunting me as I desperately tried to break free and return to Earth. I cried out as blackness swirled through the white mist—*Darkness.*

I was such an idiot! I didn't know what I was doing. I was playing with a power I had no control over.

The wisdom of the Druids will stay my hand and the Light of the Naturals will guide me home. The rope!

I reached through the nothingness, screaming for Elijah.

The tether illuminated, shimmering blue as the Druid emerged from the darkness, his hand outstretched.

He looks like an angel, I thought. *A beautiful, wingless angel.*

His hand wrapped around my wrist and our prisms ignited, then light burst through the shadow and Camelot reappeared.

I gasped and began to cough, my breath catching in my lungs. As tears sprung into my eyes, I was vaguely aware that Greer and Ramona were standing at the end of the room, staring at us in horror.

"What are you doing?" the Inquisitor demanded.

"You were *dead*," Ramona exclaimed, rushing over to Elijah and me.

"Lucky I tied that thread to you, huh?" the Druid quipped.

Ramona clucked her tongue and began to check my vitals. I swatted her away and sat up, wiping the back of my hand across my clammy brow.

"I spoke to her," I said with a scowl. "I spoke to Morgana. *The bitch*. She played us. I'm such an idiot!"

Elijah's expression dropped and he cupped my cheek to calm me. "What did she say?"

"We were right," I murmured, beginning to tremble. "She left a piece of herself behind, that's why the Flames aren't waking."

"Where? How?" he asked.

"The One. She made him anew, but this time, she put her heart into his body. She lives on in a new manifestation of Darkness."

The horrors of the past were being resurrected. If the One woke, he could create a whole new legion of demons, and if he took me, Earth, Thríbhís Mhór, and Avalon would be the first to fall.

Elijah cursed under his breath in Gaelic.

Ramona gasped and shook her head. "*It can't be.*"

Greer fell to her knees beside me and took my hand. "What do we need to do? Where is he?"

"Ben Nevis," Elijah stated, his brow furrowing. "He's inside the mountain."

"A place where only one person can enter." I leaned into his hand and sighed. "*Me.*"

"The Naturals are at your command," Greer said. "We will march to Ben Nevis together."

"No." I shook my head and squeezed her hand. "The Naturals have been through enough tragedy." I took her other hand and sighed. "I don't blame you for what happened to Issac, Greer. I'm hurting, just like everyone else, but this… Morgana… The One is her endgame now, and she made the rules so I was the only one who could face him."

"Spirit walker," Elijah murmured.

"A fifty-fifty chance."

"A fifty-fifty chance?" Ramona asked. "What does that mean?"

Greer sniffed and pulled me into her arms. "It means he could use your Triune to destroy us all, or you can defeat him and sever Morgana's hold over us once and for all."

"Who would have thought it'd come to this?" I snorted and looked at Camelot over her shoulder. "Certainly not me."

"We believe in you," Greer told me, but I didn't have it in me to reply.

Issac died so we could live, and now I had to honour his life and bring this war to an end.

It was my destiny, after all.

18

The sun rose over Camelot, its rays shining down on the ruined city through a clear sky.

Snow and ice sparkled as we walked through base camp, the winter wonderland beautiful, but the mood was sombre at best.

Greer left us, not wanting to be present when I departed—she'd been through a great deal with not only the loss of the Codex and the Twin Flames, and the duty she bore as protector and acting Inquisitor, but the loss of Issac as well. She was the strongest woman I knew, but her burdens were just as great as mine had been, if not more. Greer took on the fate of an entire people and asked for nothing in return. Seeing me leave, knowing that I may not come back was more than she could take.

Ramona returned to the infirmary, determined to make sure I had the right supplies with me when I descended into the mountain. I knew she wanted a moment to shed a tear, but I didn't bring it up, letting her have her moment in private.

Everyone dealt with loss and pain in different ways, and I had to allow them that…and understand why. It seemed important that me of all people, had the foresight to give them what they needed.

Trent and Maisy were waiting for Elijah and me outside the infirmary. It seemed like an age since I'd seen them, and our easy conversations in the kitchens felt like they were memories from another life.

"Madeleine," Trent said, his breath vaporising in the chilled air. "What's going on?"

"Are you okay?" Maisy asked.

"I have to go to Ben Nevis," I told them. "Morgana's heart lies within the mountain. That's why the Flames aren't waking. It has to be destroyed." It didn't seem like the right moment to bring up the One. If I succeeded, they never needed to know how close we came to another cataclysm.

"We're coming with you," Trent said, his expression fierce.

"You don't have to face this alone," Maisy added. "We're with you all the way to the end, Madeleine."

I felt an overwhelming urge to cry, but I steadied myself. "I know you would, but Morgana made sure I was the only one who could find it. Besides, you've all been through enough, don't you think?"

Tent took a step towards me, his hand tightening around the pommel of his arondight blade. "But—"

"I know," I said, my throat tightening. "*I know.*"

Maisy's bottom lip trembled. She was a fierce

warrior, but to me, she'd always be the girl who I'd shared a room with my first year at the Academy. Sometimes I forgot about those early days when things were at their purest. As we'd grown older, she'd fallen in with the popular crowd and I'd become bully fodder, but that was a long time ago. Now she was a sister to me, and Trent was the goofy brother I never thought I needed.

"I won't be long," I told them, hoping I was right. "And when I come back, Wilder and Scarlett will be awake."

"You'll miss Issac's funeral…" she began.

My heart twisted. "I'll give him my own send off when I get back. He'd like that."

"Good luck, Madeleine," Trent murmured, "though you don't need it. If anyone can do this, it's you."

Maisy nodded and I pulled them both in for a hug.

"Thank you for being my friends," I whispered. "I don't know if I ever told you guys that."

"I'm not crying," Maisy said, pulling away. *"I'm not crying."*

Elijah stirred behind us. He'd remained silent until now, letting us have our moment.

"If it's all the same to you," he said, "may I have a moment with my *leannán?*"

Trent and Maisy made a hasty exit, leaving us alone.

The camp around us was strangely empty—most Naturals were out assessing the damage to the city and completing their reconnaissance of the surrounding area, including the human villages which bordered the hills. There would be no fanfare when I left Camelot, but that's the way I wanted it.

"*Madeleine.*" Elijah pressed his forehead against mine and twisted his fingers through my hair.

"This is our reality," I murmured. "We were given these gifts so we could protect others."

"I knew returning with you would be difficult, but I never thought it would feel like this."

I curled my fingers into the front of his shirt and breathed in his scent. I committed all of him to memory, even the fine lines of the runes carved into his skin.

"Maybe I wasn't made by accident, but destiny. I'm okay with it, Elijah. I really am. I'm doing this not because I have to, but because I love you *and everyone.* Sacrifices have to be made for the good of the world."

"I know, but I want to be selfish. *I want to keep you.*"

He kissed me then, slow and deep, and I almost let him convince me. I had to force myself to pull away.

"If I don't come back—"

"Don't say that," he rasped. "*Please.*"

"If I don't come back," I said firmly, "I want you to go home. I want you to be with your people and your sister. *Promise me.*"

He shook his head. "I don't need to make any promises because you're coming back."

"All the more reason to humour me." I pouted. "I fought that relic so you'd have the chance to go back to Thríbhís Mhór one day. Don't tell me I did it for nothing, because that fight was *hard*."

"I know, but at least let me come with you as far as Fort William," he argued.

"*Elijah*. This is hard enough as it is. If I let you come to Ben Nevis with me, I may not have the courage to go in there."

He sighed, wiping at a stray tear. "Okay, I promise."

"*Ádh mór*," I whispered.

"I'm supposed to say that to you," he told me.

"I love you, Elijah."

"And I love you."

We clutched one another for a moment longer, our prisms humming gently.

"I'll wait for you here," he murmured. "And when you return, we'll find the nearest willow tree."

I smiled and held him close. "It's a deal."

It was a lonely road to Ben Nevis in the middle of winter.

The days were shorter in the far north of the United Kingdom—the sun set at half-past three in the afternoon.

Above, the sky was dusted with stars and within them, a soft rainbow of an aurora shimmered like a holographic curtain. It reminded me of the Druids and I fancied they were offering me their support

from the homeland in the only way they could—
through nature itself.

I stood there looking up at the summit and asked
myself the question that up until this point, I didn't
want to face.

*If the Dark was gone, why did I still have my Dark
Triune?*

Because Morgana still clung to reality, that's why. I
was going into that mountain, knowing it was likely a
suicide mission. If I killed the One, then I'd be killing
a part of my soul.

Morgana's twisted end had finally come to light.
If she couldn't possess the Triune, then no one could
—not even me.

My life for billions of others across countless
worlds. Seemed like a fair trade.

Scarlett and Wilder had faced the same odds
when they'd descended into the rift, knowing their
fight may be their end. I snorted at the irony.

My boots crunched on the snow and gravel as I
followed the trail towards the summit. I'd have to
carve a new path up ahead to find the hidden
entrance, but for now, the going was easy enough.

I lingered at the top of the rise, spotting the cave
opening through a shimmer of Dark. My lip curled
into a sneer—*a cork in the arsehole of the world.* A demon
was growing in there, harbouring the heart of a
monster and protected by the last bastion of
Darkness. Like an infestation of parasites, they just
wouldn't go away.

Taking out the quartz crystal Ramona had

tearfully thrust into my hand before I left Camelot, I held it close. My parents travelled with me through their invention, lighting my way through the shadows and masking my path from any creatures lurking where they could not be seen.

I scrambled up the icy incline and lingered outside the cave. Giving one last look at the aurora above, I stepped into the shadow of the mountain.

Shadow surrounded me, making my path treacherous, but I didn't dare cast light out into the tunnel. After a few twists and turns, I began to sense I wasn't alone.

Rusting echoed through the dark, and otherworldly clicks and screeches found their way to my ears. Soon the sounds were all around me, haunting my every step.

They knew I was here.

It was no use hiding and scratching in the dark. Holding out my palm, I gathered a little orb of Light and sent it bobbing up into the air.

I gasped as the horror of what grew inside Ben Nevis was revealed. Black, slimy, twisted demons were everywhere.

The light shone off silver eyes and made black hides glow. Everywhere I turned, hideous demonic faces peered at me, snarling and snapping as I edged by. Razor-sharp claws and pointed teeth flashed as I turned, my heartbeat speeding up to impossible levels.

The Dark had been destroyed, but these creatures were newborns. The One was creating a new legion of demons to replace the ones Morgana's death had taken. I was witnessing the birth of a new race.

My hand brushed against my arondight blade, but I resisted the urge to unsheathe it. Why weren't they attacking? Their first and only desire was to consume with chaotic abandon, so why were they keeping to the shadows? They were formed enough to know hunger…

I sighed and bit my bottom lip.

They wanted me to go to the One.

Squashing down the urge to throw up, I kept moving. The tunnels began to warm the deeper I climbed, the floors uneven and slippery with condensation. Little clumps of mineral crystals grew in divots and cracks, shimmering white and pink like clusters of salt.

Finally, I passed through a fissure that looked an awful lot like an extinct volcanic tube—a long cooled conduit lava used to flow through on its way to the surface. Ben Nevis was an ancient volcano, but a few billion years had passed since the mountain had blown itself to pieces.

I ran my fingers over the walls, knowing that extinct wasn't a barrier when it came to Morgana. She'd proven that in Edinburgh.

My senses drew me along the ancient conduit, and I scrambled down the decline and passed into a large pocket of stale air.

The cavern was huge. The sound of dripping condensation echoed through the hollow, the minerals grew massive stalagmites and stalactites that reached towards each other like ghostly fingers.

I froze, my gaze falling on a large mass of writhing Darkness. It shuddered and moved, squirming like a growing child in a womb. Legs, arms, the roundness of a head, toes, fingers…

This was it. The One. He was waiting to be born, but who knew if it was me he needed to wake. It didn't matter how or why. I was here to kill him before he could open his eyes and take his first breath. I was here to destroy Morgana's heart.

You are capable of more than you realise. Both Celestials had told me as much, but I was only now beginning to realise what they meant.

I approached the mass, my Light shining through its translucent skin. I could see through forming flesh and stretching bones, right into the centre of its being where a twisted black heart beat slowly.

Ba-boom. Ba-Boom. Ba-boom.

I shook my head as the sound pierced my Dark Triune. The power of the One was growing, its essence strange yet intoxicating.

Enough! I snapped out of it and gathered my whole Triune.

Time slowed around me as I left my physical body behind. It was becoming easier to walk into the place between life and death—a thought that kind of frightened me a little.

I reached a ghostly hand into the formless creature and curled my fingers around the beating black blob within. It was sticky to the touch, like thick tar with the stench to match.

So this was Morgana's twisted heart. She was right about one thing—when she took on her human form, something broke inside her. Her core had festered, poisoning everything she touched.

I held the Celestial's heart in my hand and felt her spirit call out to me.

We could rule the universe together… Morgana's voice echoed through her link to the One. *Nothing can stand in our way. You and I can ascend past the Celestials and reach the Old Ones…*

Lies, my soul cried out. *You thought this was going to be a battle to the death? That I'd have to fight between my so-called paths to destiny? You underestimated me, Morgana. I don't need a sword to fight you! I have the one thing you never did.*

Power is all I need, she shouted through the void. *Power and blood.*

You're wrong, I told her. *It's love. Unconditional and complete love.*

Then you are a fool, Madeleine Greenbriar. Love will always betray you in the end.

She was wrong. Love made up the ties that bound all living things together. The Naturals, the Druids, humanity, and all the creatures of the Earth. Love gave us true power to live peacefully. Love was everything—a journey, a pact, peace. Love was life itself.

I feel sorry for you, Morgana, I said. *I understood what you meant when you said you and I are the same. We were both broken by accident by other's good intentions, but that's where it ends. I chose to embrace my broken and turn it into love. You chose to wield yours with hate, betraying your true nature as a Celestial.* I stared at her heart, pitying the blackened thing she'd become. *I'm sorry, Morgana, but I can't help you.*

Don't, the Celestial cried. *Madeleine…*

I shook my head, my spirit shimmering in the deepest part of the mountain. The Earth sang to me, my loved ones calling me home. I understood I wouldn't be there for long, but if I didn't do this, they'd cease to be.

The One began to stir, unfolding his shadowy limbs and opened his jaws. He bore down on my physical body and I had no choice. *I struck.*

I closed my fist around Morgana's heart, crushing the twisted organ in my hand like a rotten piece of fruit.

The spirit realm shattered around me, the force throwing me back into my body as my soul shrieked. My Dark Triune sparked erratically, fire erupting along every nerve ending.

I screamed in agony, my cries answered by the Dark things which lingered in the mountain as the One shuddered and began to collapse in on himself.

As I fell to the ground, gasping for breath, I knew I was in deep trouble.

It seemed I was right about one thing at least.

I'd just lost part of my soul.

19

I was alive, but barely.

Ben Nevis shuddered around me, the earth quaking as the One imploded. I couldn't move as I watched him suck all the light out of the chamber.

Rock began to split, the caves collapsing in on themselves. The dark places the demons had carved out for themselves were disintegrating with the One. If I didn't get out of here, I'd be crushed.

This wasn't how I was meant to die.

Reaching deep within myself, I found a shred of my remaining Triune and pulled. A flicker of strength pulsed in my limbs and I clung to it with everything I had. I felt my way across the cavern, fumbling in the dark while my body screamed in agony.

The mountain shuddered, casting a shower of rock and grit down on me. Finally, I made it from the cavern and into the volcanic tube.

I cried out as a demon landed next to me, but its silver gaze was vacant. I scrambled past it as the creature began to dissolve, bubbling and spitting as if acid was eating it from the inside out.

I forged on, hope guiding me to the light. It may have been misguided, but at least I couldn't be crushed inside a mountain of Darkness. At least I would see the sky one last time…

The last gasp of the Darkness shuddered through me. I should have rejoiced. Centuries of war and turmoil were finally over for good. The Naturals were free. The Lady of the Lake was safe. The Druids… I was numb to the triumph of victory.

All the newborn demons were dead, and I was the only living thing that breathed inside the peak. I was alone as I clawed my way through the twisting tunnels, desperately searching for the exit.

I wanted my parents—my mother's gentle touch and my father's awful jokes.

I wanted Elijah's cringe-worthy one-liners and undying love.

I wanted my friends and my home.

I wanted Camelot.

The crystal was warm in my hand as I drew on the last of my strength and called on my prism. It flared, pushing me the last few feet towards the exit, but just as suddenly as its Colour flowed through me, it severed.

I stumbled, tumbling out of the mountain and into the snow. My connection… Elijah… *He was gone…*

Empty sobs took the last of my strength as I lay in the cold, numb and alone.

I was dying.

I didn't have to be a genius to understand the mind could not live without the soul. The foundation of my Triune was gone and without it, the rest of me would collapse into a fractured mess. I would shatter and float in nothingness for eternity.

At least I wouldn't be conscious. There was a silver lining, no matter how shite it seemed.

May the Light guide you to eternal peace.

My sword arm jarred as my blade clashed with heavy steel. I twisted, bringing my blade around in an arc and was countered again. This time I locked with my opponent, our skill matched.

"You'll have to do better than that." My gaze met Issac's and I grinned. "I was top of my class in swordplay, you know."

"I don't doubt it," he quipped, breaking our deadlock.

Metal scraped against metal as we broke apart, the training yard in Camelot shimmering through a veil of illusion. The practice sword was heavy in my hand, the unfamiliar feel of regular steel an annoying weight. Cold iron was ten times lighter than this, but a weighty and dull blade was good for building upper body strength.

"You're a little sluggish today," Issac said, wiping the sweat off his brow. "Are you feeling all right."

"Yes, I guess." I shrugged. "I'm kind of dying

right now. I'm glad it's summer again, though. I always liked Camelot at this time of year. There's no mud."

Issac chuckled, the sound of his laughter a comfort to my fraying soul

I looked at him, studying the memory of his annoyingly clean-cut handsomeness. The way he styled his hair in an artful swept back swoosh. How his T-shirt clung to his lean muscles. The flash of his clear eyes and the hard lines of his jaw.

I preferred how he'd let go of his put-together look and became a little more scruffy around the edges, but this was how I remembered him best—strong, well adjusted, grown up, sensible. *Issac*.

"You're not real, are you?" I asked him.

He smiled. "You know I'm not."

"Way to dash my hopes." I set down my practice sword. "It would have been nice to see the end of all things with you."

Issac's expression fell. "I can't say that it's that poetic. I imagine it just stops."

Lowering my gaze, I scuffed the tip of my boot in the dust. "I wonder what will happen to my soul when it shatters?"

"You already know the answer to that question," he said. "And we both know that's not why your mind brought you here. What aren't you asking yourself, Madeleine?"

"I guess I wanted to say goodbye." I looked up at him as tears gathered in my eyes. "You were torn away so fast…I never got the chance to say anything."

He waited for me to gather my thoughts.

"I know why you had to," I went on, "but it hurt, Issac."

"Life isn't easy. It's full of pain and suffering, yet we protect it anyway. Why is that?"

"I can't believe my subconscious is giving me a lecture right now," I grumbled.

"Why, Madeleine?"

"Because life is also full of wonder. There is beauty amongst pain. There's love."

"Well, I did teach you something after all." Issac smiled and his image began to fade. "You'll do just fine…"

"Wait!" I took a step forwards, my heart skipping a beat. "I'm not ready yet! *Issac!*"

I opened my eyes.

Above, the aurora brightened into rippling sheets of greens and blues. Stars shone through the veil of colour, twinkling with the power of the universe.

It was a beautiful sight to behold at the end of my short and tumultuous life. I was glad I was able to look upon something so pure before I was cast into the abyss.

I gasped for breath as my mind began to peel away from my flesh. The frosty air and snow beneath me had long sent my fingers and toes numb, so I didn't feel much at all.

The crystal had fallen to the ground, but I felt the

faint pulse of its energy nearby—the last connection I had with home.

The aurora faded into a sheet of violet and silver, then rippled back to brilliant emerald. I stared up at the twisting light and said a silent prayer.

At least I wasn't alone. The stars were a comfort.

A gust of wind fluttered my hair and Wilder knelt beside me, his Flame simmering.

"She's fading," he said, his voice muffled like he was talking underwater. "Part of her soul is gone…"

"I was afraid of this," Scarlett said, appearing on the other side, her indigo hair swirling in the breeze. "Oh, you brave girl… We're so proud of you."

"Elijah," I whispered. "*I want Elijah…*"

Her brow furrowed.

"The Druid," Wilder told her. "She loves him."

"Then we better get her home," she replied.

Words tried to form in my throat, but I couldn't speak.

Scarlett smiled and took my hand in hers. Her skin was warm as her Light poured into me and I didn't dare hope. *Was she real?*

"Merry Christmas, Madeleine," she said before she lifted me up into the heavens. "It's time to go home."

20

I made my peace.

I'd saved everyone and the Earth was safe… and so were the Druids. Still, I lingered.

Was it false hope or a stubborn will to live? I didn't know.

The air carried the haunting scent of lilac and primrose, and the familiar perfume coaxed my eyes open.

I expected to see the absence of everything—the white void where I found Morgana—but I stood on top of a hill. A lush, emerald green forest stretched into the valley below, shimmering with refracted light, and the lake beyond rippled with colour.

Avalon.

I turned as I sensed someone approach and stilled as the Lady of the Lake stepped gracefully towards me, appearing out of the haze like a shining beacon. Her white dress flowed around her, shimmering with starlight and her hair glowed with the power of a thousand galaxies.

"Lady?"

"Morgana is no more," she murmured, sitting gracefully on the ground. "I mourn for her loss, but I understand why it must be so." She bade me to sit beside her and when I did, I realised Avalon was an illusion.

"We're not really here, are we?"

"No. This is merely a vision…an echo inside your memories."

I sighed and looked up at the pink sky. "I'm still dying, aren't I? You're not really here, either."

"On the contrary," the Celestial said, "I am real and here to fulfil a promise I made to you, Madeleine."

"If you could help, you would…"

She nodded, her silver hair shimmering.

"You've come to help me pass into the next life?"

"Your soul is damaged from the loss of one of your Triunes," she explained. "You are fading, but for now, you rest in a deep sleep amongst friends."

"Amongst friends?" I echoed, confused.

"You rest within Glastonbury," she told me, "where Avalon was taken from. My Flames took you from Morgana's mountain and carried you home."

"Avalon is a piece of Glastonbury?" I wondered, skipping over all the important parts.

The Lady laughed and gesture to the valley below. "Two thousand years ago, this place was teeming with life. Human clans waged wars, fighting for pride and freedom as they do now, but we were all safe here on the Isle. Then the Romans came, and everything changed. Glastonbury closed its doors to outsiders, I removed a piece to create the haven of Avalon, the Druids became secretive, and the first Naturals were born. It was a tumultuous time."

I edged closer to her, eager to hear more. There was so little we knew about our origins as Naturals.

"These Isles are full of ancient power," she continued. "They are ancient, connected to the stars and to the ether of the Earth. All realities have such a place."

"Is that why you created the Naturals?" I asked. "To protect the land against the invading Romans?"

"In part," she admitted. "But it was more than that. My family had already been on this Earth for thousands of years, watching it grow. My parents succumbed to their physical bodies and passed into the spirit world and I was alone. I couldn't protect the Isles on my own and…"

"You were lonely," I murmured.

"I knew there were others out there, but I didn't know how to find them and…I was afraid of leaving and not being able to find my way back. Earth was all I knew."

"But you can ascend," I told her. "You were born, but you earned your path back to the stars. You're still a Celestial no matter how you were created. You could have gone *home*."

The Lady shook her head, her hair shimmering. "I have not earned transcendence."

"I don't understand…"

"Your people worship a false prophet," she whispered.

I blinked, bewildered at her rising tears. "The Naturals are your people, Lady. You created us."

"I did, but instead of nurturing you, I led you onto a path of destruction."

"I don't understand," I said. "You're not responsible for this. We all played a part."

It took her a moment to gather her thoughts, so we sat together, watching the vision of Avalon ripple in the distance.

"I watched over the Naturals for centuries," she began. "Then I saw a man rise to power, who held such charisma and essence…" Her expression became misty as she remembered him and I realised she'd been in love with him. "That was the moment everything changed."

"Who was he?" I asked.

"Arthur Pendragon."

"Arthur?" I whispered.

The Lady was lost in her story and continued without elaborating, "The Naturals had built their great city in the hills and valleys. They reigned supreme, yet in harmony with all of Earth's creations. But outside Camelot's walls, the human world was one of suffering and turmoil. Wars raged across the entire world, driven by greed and lust for power. Holy wars fought over religions but brimming with sins. The bloodshed drew Morgana's gaze and drawn by my influence, she came looking for me."

"That's when you asked Merlin to help you imprison her underneath Camelot," I remarked. "He advised the Naturals, so he was the conduit for your will."

"You are perceptive, Madeleine," the Lady said. "In the weeks after Morgana's imprisonment, I gave Arthur the gift of Excalibur. Then to his greatest knight, Lancelot, I gave Arondight. Together, they would help steer the world onto a better path. A peaceful one full of tolerance and understanding. I hoped harmony would return and nature would bloom…and Morgana would return, with pure starlight once more."

I frowned, knowing it hadn't quite worked out that way. Morgana had only festered, for one. And humans weren't creations of any supreme being—at least not that we knew—and they guided themselves, driven by the primal forces of nature…and their easily swayed hearts.

"But you were still lonely, weren't you?"

The Lady nodded. "My children revered my name, yet I was apart from them. They carved statues of my likeness out of marble and precious stone. They prayed to me morning and night. They named their children in my honour. But I wanted to be amongst the knights and ladies as their equal. I wanted to walk their city and feel the grass between my toes…so I descended from Avalon, but I couldn't go as the Lady of the Lake. I couldn't be one with them when they set me apart, so I became one of them."

The Lady of the Lake had taken on Natural form —a disguise—so she could connect with someone. It was a sorrowful tale and I couldn't help but feel a connection with it. To be amongst a crowded life, yet apart from it.

"I wasn't prepared for how human I'd become," the Lady murmured. "I fell in love. Deep, passionate love…with two men."

I froze, the truth of what she'd done drove a terrible pain through my heart. *Guinevere.*

"Now you see why I cannot ascend," she whispered as a shimmering tear fell from her eye. "I created the calamity that tore apart the world I loved so dearly. I was the reason the Dark came. Arthur and Lancelot crossed Excalibur and Arondight in hatred over their love for me, and the world tore in two."

"But what about your son?" I asked. "What about Mordred?"

"Mordred…" Her starlight flickered, and I felt her pain pass through Avalon and into the spirit world where we sat, drawn together by fate. "I couldn't save Arthur. He'd leapt into the rift before I could stop him and Lancelot… I could not save them, but I could try to protect my unborn child."

I knew what happened next, but it wasn't my story to tell.

"While the child grew, I was trapped in my Natural form, unable to return to Avalon. I was captured by a demon named Eilhana…" She lowered her gaze and her shoulders began to shake with silent sobs.

Eilhana. The memory of the power the name had once held over me was a barbed echo. She was the demon who'd put a piece of herself into Mordred, and in turn, had become my Dark Triune.

"She tortured you, took your child, and turned him into a monster," I murmured.

We sat in silence, looking over the vision of Avalon with heavy hearts. All she wanted was to connect with someone and it had led to so much suffering. Guinevere's heart was broken. Should I be angry with her? Pity her? Curse her for eternity? I didn't know.

Finally, she spoke. "Merlin helped me escape. Together, we travelled to Avalon and did what we could to ensure the return of the Naturals and the safety of the Druids. I was weakened without Excalibur and Arondight, but I returned to my Celestial form and together, we made our plot to save the Earth. Together, they could right the wrongs I'd done where I could not. That is the truth, Madeleine. I am not a goddess or saviour. I'm just a silly girl who fell in love."

Now I understood why love was so important in everything the Naturals did, and why it was so ingrained in our Light. It was a difficult lesson, and Guinevere had learned it the hard way.

I didn't hate her. How could I? Love tore us apart, but it also brought us back together.

"It's over now," I told her. "Morgana is gone and the Dark with her. The Twin Flames sealed the rift, and now the Naturals can rebuild Camelot. You helped us, Guinevere. Without you, we would have failed."

She smiled and took my hand. "You are sweet, Madeleine. Perhaps you are right, but I will always carry the scar of what I've done. You are here, suffering, because of what I did so long ago. All of us are connected and our actions ripple through time, changing everything they touch."

I stared at her, not understanding what she was trying to say. But maybe it wasn't a matter of understanding, but not wanting to hear her words.

"The time of the Celestials is over," Guinevere said. "Our people were wrong to take on flesh and bone. We were wrong to interfere in mortal affairs, but what's done is done. There is no taking it back. My only hope is that my children can do better in the dawning of a new age." She was giving us her truth so we could begin anew and create our own destiny.

I shook my head, my throat tightening. "But without you, the Naturals will die like the Dark did with Morgana. *Guinevere…*"

"Do not fret," she murmured. "You will live on, Madeleine. It is my final gift to you. Please do me the honour of accepting." She held out her free hand and I watched in awe as her palm filled with transcendent stardust. It shimmered silver and brilliant, vibrating with the essence of the universe.

"I give you my starlight so you can live, Madeleine Greenbriar. I give it to you above all others; you, who scarified so much to save so many. Will you accept?"

"But… I…" My hands began to tremble. "Are you asking me to become part Celestial?"

Guinevere nodded. "I am."

I sucked in a sharp breath. I hardly seemed a worthy candidate, especially considering the Lady of the Lake was offering her life so I could live. "But wouldn't that mean I'd become immortal?"

"It would, but you already had a semblance of prolonged life when your Triune was intact."

I stared at her life force as it sparkled in her outstretched hand.

She smiled, understanding my hesitation. "When the time comes where you wish to return to Earth, you will be able to pass your gifts on to another. Forever is a burden no one should have to shoulder."

"I…" I swallowed hard, "I accept."

Guinevere took my hand and closed it over hers, her starlight pulsing as it began to merge with a new life.

"I name you Cerridwen, the Flame of Wisdom… for my mother," she murmured. "May wisdom and Light shine within you to guide your people into the future."

"Was that her name?" I asked as her starlight flowed into me. "Cerridwen?"

Guinevere nodded. "It was the name the people of the lands we settled in gave her. It is in their language, for we had none of our own. My father was Tegid, and my true name…Creirwy." She smiled, lost in memory. "Yes, that was what they named me."

"Creirwy," I murmured.

"I give you my wisdom, my secrets, and my essence," she whispered. "And I give you Avalon. Use them well, Madeleine Greenbriar. May the Light guide you to eternal glory…"

Warmth spread through my body as Guinevere began to shimmer. Her translucent skin began to fade, sparkling with trillions of points of powerful starlight.

The Lady of the Lake dissolved into stardust. I held out my hand as the last of her essence trailed off into the depths of the spirit world, carried away by the currents of fate.

"*Slán*, Guinevere," I murmured. "*Ádh mór…*"

21

———

When I opened my eyes, the room was dappled with a fine layer of stardust.

I lay in a bed surrounded by beeping machines and silver walls. I breathed deeply and blinked, focusing on a body lounging in a chair beside me.

Elijah.

As I stared at him, he shone with Colour, his runes rippling with blue and silver threads.

I couldn't fathom what I was seeing, let alone feeling. I possessed a *knowing*, a sixth sense. It was as if I stood a second earlier in front of everyone else, one foot in the future and one in the present. All the layers of the world were peeled back, and I could see inside and around all that lived and was.

"My *leannán*..." I murmured, reaching for him.

"Madeleine!" The Druid shot to his feet and took my hand. "*You're awake*. They said you lost your Dark Triune..." He sat on the bed beside me and stroked my hair.

I stared at him, transfixed by the swirling Colours twisting and turning over his skin. His eyes were iridescent emerald as they searched mine. He'd spoken, but the words didn't register.

"You're beautiful," I whispered. "*Rwy'n dy garu di*."

His brow creased and he brushed his palm across my forehead, checking my temperature. "Are you high again? You're speaking Welsh."

"She came to me," I murmured. "The Lady of the Lake."

He paused. "When?"

"While I floated between life and death." His fingers were warm as they clutched my hand and I wondered if he could feel Guinevere's gift. "She gave me her starlight so I could come back…" I brushed my fingers over his cheek, passing my knowledge to him.

Elijah's eyes widened and filled with tears. "*Mo dhia…* Madeleine."

"Are they here?" I asked. "Are the Flames awake?"

Elijah nodded. "Wilder and Scarlett picked you up off the side of Ben Nevis and brought you here."

"I thought it was a dream," I murmured, the light hurting my eyes.

"No," he whispered, cupping my face with a trembling hand. "It is not a dream, Cerridwen…the Flame of Wisdom."

Emotion welled inside me and I sat up so I could draw Elijah to me. "She…Guinevere gave me her soul so I could live."

"I can see it," he told me. "Your eyes… They're not grey anymore."

"They aren't?"

"They're blue, green…" he smiled and traced his fingertip along the curve of my cheek and across the soft skin under my eye, "violet…and I can see strands of silver. They're like a galaxy burning brightly in the heavens."

I snorted and began to laugh, the warmth of life flowing back into my weary bones. "Elijah the poet. Perhaps we can find you a new profession after all."

He smiled and his runes shimmered. I wondered if he could see them like I did, but I thought it was unlikely. I pressed my palm on his arm and the prism I'd given him flared back to life, the iridescent threads crawling up his arm. My own prism answered, linking us once more.

Elijah gazed into my eyes, his lips inching towards mine. "You really are a marvel, Madeleine Greenbriar."

As we were about to kiss, the door flew open and collided with the wall. I jerked back from Elijah and stared in amusement as Scarlett Ravenwood flew into the room like a tornado of Indigo Flame.

"Madeleine!" she shouted to anyone who would listen. "She's awake! *Madeleine's awake!*"

As usual, Arondight had perfect timing.

A new year dawned, and with it came a new age.

I sat on the cliff overlooking the keep, the icy wind tugging at my black hair.

Below, Camelot was a hive of activity, even at the hour before the sun even rose. It was the dead of winter and still dark at eight a.m., but it didn't give the Naturals a free pass to sleep in. Not even on New Year's Day.

Everyone had something to do and were as equally excited to get started.

Aiden had reopened the archive and restoration had already begun, fuelled by the enthusiastic archeological team—with Amanda firmly beside him at all times. He'd said that now, more than ever, was the time to begin preserving our history and writing the next chapter of Camelot's story.

And his brother, Thompson, was currently restructuring security. Since there were no more demons to protect the city against, his job had become quite leisurely. Trent and Maisy had requested to remain, much to my delight, though at the cost of Trent being offered a post at the Academy. Seemed the headmaster, Islington, had need of a new weapons professor. How the class clown pulled that off was beyond even me.

My parents had reopened their research station at the base camp and were continuing their work, applying their findings to better conceal Sanctums all round the world. Humanity was only going to grow and soon they'd encroach in on our territory, but with my parents' new illusions, we could fold ourselves into space and time, keeping our existence secret for as long as we were able. The silent protection of the Naturals would continue, helping shape the world for thousands of years to come.

I sighed and pulled the Light of the Lady award out of my coat pocket.

I turned it over in my hand, running my thumb over the jewels, lost in thought. Everyone was currently living their best lives, free of the shadows of the past, but I still had so many questions.

About my abilities, my role in this new world, my life, my longevity, and about Guinevere herself. I wanted to know who she'd been, where she'd lived, what she'd done, and why she was the Celestial she was. Her soul was a part of mine now—she was my identity.

I'd read all the stories passed down from the Welsh people and none of them made any sense, but I knew that's how myths worked. People added and embellished as they saw fit, changing a tale to make it suit their needs. But at the core of every epic, was a shred of truth.

Guinevere… *Creirwy*.

The truth was hard to find, but it always made itself known eventually. Maybe one day I'd be able to unlock the legacy inside to reach the understanding I craved. *Perhaps…*

A gust of wind buffeted me and I sensed Arondight land gracefully on the cliff top. Indigo Flame brushed against my starlight and I smiled.

"There you are," Scarlett said, flopping down beside me. "I've been looking for you everywhere."

"I needed a little room to breathe," I admitted. "It's bright even in the middle of the night."

She tilted her head to the side. "It's a trip, isn't it?"

"Auras," I mused, "sound, thought, the currents of time. It's all so loud."

"Well, the aura thing I can relate to, but the currents of time?" She whistled and kicked her legs over the side of the cliff and swung them back and forth. "I'm sorry to admit that time travel is a little beyond the Indigo Flame."

"It is a little overwhelming."

"I bet Elijah has a rune for that," she mused. "Don't forget you're Druid compatible."

"I'll ask him."

"You did good with that one," Scarlett quipped. "Sexy, brooding, reformed bad boy, *tattooed*." She fanned herself.

"And completely mine."

"I know. I've got a bad boy of my own." She laughed, the sound so infectious, I found myself grinning. That was Scarlett, though—she thrived as Arondight.

"I'm glad I can be here with you," I told her. "I was afraid we'd have to take turns in Avalon."

"Well, I would like to see it again someday, and I think Wilder would want to check it out eventually."

"It's not a resort, you know."

"You could make bank, just saying," was her amused reply. "Anyway, your Natural and Druid Triunes balance out the Celestial. I wouldn't worry about anyone falling into comas. We always flapped on about the balance between Light and Dark, and this is just another set of weights. *All good.*"

Celestial. It was strange to think that Guinevere was a part of me now, especially considering her past relationship with Arthur and Lancelot was linked to Wilder and Scarlett—another sort of Triune.

"I really am going to live forever now," I murmured.

"Not if you chose to pass your Flame on," she reminded me. "Wilder and I are one thing, but you, Madeleine…you seriously levelled up."

"I'm going to have to ask Jackson to explain some of these gamer references," I said.

"Oh, did you hear? Esme had her baby! Only a few weeks late, mind you. Can you believe they can stay in there for longer than nine months? I couldn't handle it."

I laughed, not realising how much I'd missed her unpredictable good-humour until now. "What did they have?"

"A girl," she said with a moan. "Jackson's in for it, I tell you."

"What did they name her?"

"They can't agree on that yet."

"When do they agree on anything?"

"Exactly!" Scarlett clapped her hands together and began to laugh hysterically.

I was glad she was here.

"I missed you while you were gone," I told her.

Her laughter faded and she looked at me with

regret. "I'm sorry," she murmured. "I had a duty to the Regula."

"I know," I said. "It took me a while to understand, but I'm glad you're here with me now."

Scarlett tilted her head to the side and peered at me, her Flame simmering as mine stirred. I'm sure I'd get used to it eventually, but for now, it was still the strangest sensation.

"Greer's in a complete tizzy," she said. "You should have seen her before. If I didn't talk her down, I'm sure her head would have spun all the way around. She has to rewrite the Codex *again*. This has never happened in all the time it's been around."

I knew what she meant. Our entire history had been upended so many times over the past six years, it was ridiculous, and now it was in the midst of a seismic change.

"I can help her," I said, "like you did after your adventure."

Scarlett nodded and looked out over Camelot. "There's a lot of work to do, not just with the Codex."

"I hardly know where to begin," I admitted. "The dawning of a new age is intimidating. I hardly seem like the right candidate to guide an entire race of people into the future."

"Guinevere gave you her starlight for a reason, Madeleine," Scarlett told me. "You don't have to have all the answers. We'll work it out together. Elijah has agreed to consult with the Regula as an advisor, just as Merlin did."

"He agreed?" I asked, sitting up straight. "He was grumbling about it last night."

"He told Greer this morning. No doubt he's looking for you so he can let you know. Sorry for the spoiler."

"How far we've come…" I shook my head with a little amusement and a little disbelief mixing in for good measure.

In that moment, I wished Issac was here to see all of this. I wondered what he'd say seeing Scarlett and I atop the cliff, both of us the vessels for celestial Flame.

You're not a vessel, Madeleine, he'd say in his straightforward, know-it-all tone. *Your soul is Celestial.*

I slipped the Light of the Lady award back into my pocket and knew I'd be asking the Regula to make a new award in honour of Issac's sacrifice. It was a small gesture, but there was nothing worthy enough in this world to match the sacrifice he'd made to save us.

"It's quiet out there," I mused. "The humans seem as chaotic as usual, and the Naturals brighter than ever…and there are others, too. Other supernatural creatures lingering in the far reaches of the Earth." I looked at her, watching the light play off her indigo hair. "Can you feel them, too?"

"Yes," she replied. "Wilder and I have known there is more out there ever since we became Flames. After the rift closed, when we were learning the extent of our abilities, we found many clusters of essence. We thought it best to keep it to ourselves. They aren't hurting anyone."

"I know." I sighed and swung my boots back and

forth. "They just want to live in peace like everyone else."

We sat in silence for a while, watching the sun peek over the rise. The first rays of light played over the tips of the ruined castle, officially heralding the new age.

"I'm at a loss," I said after a moment. "I've fought my whole life and now that there's true peace, I don't know what to do."

"The Dark is gone, but this isn't the end," Scarlett told me. "Other powers will rise soon enough, and we must be there to protect this world against all of them."

I nodded. "It's the cycle of all things."

"See?" she exclaimed. "Your wisdom is manifesting already!"

I smiled, the burden lifting off my heart. When she said it like that, the future didn't seem so huge and scary. My friends would be by my side to help guide me, and Elijah's love would make my heart sing and my starlight bloom.

"Well, would you look at that?" Scarlett mused, breaking me out of my reverie.

I looked up to see an aurora shimmer in the sky above Camelot, and my breath caught. It was an echo of the beauty I'd seen above Ben Nevis—the colours rippling through a million shades of green, blue, and even purple.

Another world began to show its face through the veil—a shining lake and a forest made of emeralds… an ancient valley cut from the wilds of Britain.

"Avalon," Scarlett whispered. "The Isle of Glass…" *Ynys Wydryn*. "Are you doing that?"

"I hardly know," I whispered, staring through the curtain of colour. "Perhaps I am."

"The purple is a nice touch."

"You're welcome."

As we sat there watching Camelot come alive, my heart sang. Yes, the future wasn't so scary after all.

The Dark was gone and would no longer rise. The Druids would flourish in their homeland, guided by Merlin's wise hand. The Celestials had already begun to fade into myth, though Guinevere's legacy would never be forgotten. And finally… centuries of war were behind the Naturals. There would always be trials, but for now we could rest, rebuild, and forge the future we'd all dreamed about.

Scarlett stood and peered over the edge of the cliff. There was a wicked gleam in her eye, and I readied myself.

"Race to base camp?" she asked.

"*You're on.*"

Scarlett let out a *whoop* and dove over the edge, her Flame igniting and twisting her into the air.

I lingered, my gaze finding the last pinpricks of light in the night sky. As the stars faded and the day dawned, my heart swelled.

"Farewell, Guinevere," I murmured. "May the stars guide you to eternal peace."

Then I leapt into the air, the currents of time and space leading me home.

. . .

The end.

Dear Reader,

Thank you for reading The Camelot Archive! I hope you enjoyed Madeleine's adventure as much as I did writing it.

If you'd like to hear more from the world of the Naturals, Druids, and Celestials, they appear throughout my other series in unexpected ways.

If you would like to know more about the mysterious third Celestial, her story is told in **The Witch Hunter Saga**. The series is complete and you can currently download the first ebook for free!

If it's Druids you're interested in, Look out for **The Darkland Druids**! It tells the story of a group of Druids who became lost in the Darklands…only to find themselves on an alternate Earth with its own apocalyptic problems.

And as always, if you'd like more stories about any of my worlds or characters, please let me know. I'd love to hear from you.

- Nicole R. Taylor

nicole.this.is@gmail.com

Want more novels just like this one? Check out Nicole's other series:

THE ARONDIGHT CODEX - An ancient war with demons. A lost sword with the power to end it all. And a woman with purple hair is the world's only hope.

THE CAMELOT ARCHIVE - Set in the same alternate Arthurian world seen in **The Arondight Codex**... Deadly secrets. Murder and revenge. The end of the world is nye and Camelot is the last bastion of hope.

THE WITCH HUNTER SAGA - Vampires and witches collide in this thrilling Urban Fantasy adventure. You've never met vampires quite like these...

THE CRESCENT WITCH CHRONICLES - Witches, shapeshifters, and ancient myth collide in this colourful Irish flavoured series! Come on an adventure fraught with danger and forbidden romance... and the ultimate battle to save magic before it's gone forever.

THE DARKLAND DRUIDS - A woman with no living relatives travels from Australia to the other side of the world to find out the truth of who she is...only to land in the middle of a prophecy of destruction.

Druids, witches, fae, and shapeshifters abound in this thrilling magical adventure!

Find out more at: NicoleRTaylorWrites.com

See what titles are FREE at: Nicole's Free Reads

ABOUT NICOLE

Nicole R. Taylor is an Australian Urban Fantasy author.

She lives in the western suburbs of Melbourne dreaming up nail biting stories featuring sassy witches, duplicitous vampires, hunky shapeshifters, and devious monsters.

She likes chocolate, cat memes, and video games.

When she's not writing, she likes to think of what she's writing next.

Follow Nicole Online:

Website: www.nicolertaylorwrites.com
Facebook: facebook.com/nrtaylorwrites
Newsletter: www.nicolertaylorwrites.com/newsletter
Email: nicole.this.is@gmail.com